DATE DUE			

Smoking Mirror

Smoking Mirror

An Encounter with Paul Gauguin

DOUGLAS REES

WATSON-GUPTILL PUBLICATIONS/NEW YORK

ACKNOWLEDGMENTS

I wish to thank my friends Dan Armil, Laura Elizabeth Baugher, and Kathleen Bullene
for their help and advice in the difficult task of completing this story.
Without them, it would not exist.

Series Editor: Jacqueline Ching
Editor: Laaren Brown
Production Manager: Hector Campbell
Book Design: Jennifer Browne

First published in 2005 in the United States by Watson-Guptill Publications,
a division of VNU Business Media, Inc.,
770 Broadway, New York, NY 10003
www.wgpub.com

Front cover: Paul Gauguin (1848-1903), *Matamoe, or Peacocks in the Country*, 1892. Oil on
canvas, 45.2 x 33.8 in (115 x 86 cm). Pushkin Museum of Fine Arts, Moscow. Photo by Erich
Lessing/Art Resource, New York. Back cover: Portrait of Paul Gauguin, 1893 © Snark
Archives/Art Resource, New York. Chapter art from *2001 Decorative Cuts and Ornaments*,
edited by Carol Belanger Grafton © 1988 by Dover Publications, Inc.

Library of Congress Cataloging-in-Publication Data
Smoking mirror : an encounter with Paul Gauguin / by Douglas Rees.
p. cm. — (Art encounters)
Summary: in Tahiti in the 1890s, sixteen-year-old Joe, a native Californian and a sailor, deter-
mines to avenge the death of his best friend at the hands of a gun smuggler known as The
White Wolf, and finds an unlikely ally in the artist, Paul Gauguin.
ISBN 0-8230-4863-2
1. Gauguin, Paul, 1848-1903—Juvenile fiction. [1. Gauguin, Paul, 1848-1903—Fiction. 2.
Tahiti—History—19th century—Fiction. 3. Artists—Fiction. 4. Friendship—Fiction. 5.
Revenge—Fiction. 6. Conduct of life—Fiction. 7. Adventure and adventurers—Fiction.]
I. Title. II. Series.
PZ7.R25475Sm 2005 [Fic]—dc22 2004009660

This book was set in Stempel Garamond.

Printed in the U.S.A.
First printing, 2005
1 2 3 4 5 6 7 8 9 / 12 11 10 09 08 07 06 05

For Judith

Contents

Preface

"I close my eyes in order to see."

So said Paul Gauguin about his paintings of the beautiful tropical islands and exotic, mysterious, natives who look out from them.

When Paul Gauguin arrived in Tahiti for the first time in 1891, he found it to be a very different place from the one he would come to make famous through his art. It was not an exotic paradise full of unspoiled primitive people. That Tahiti had existed once, but regular contact with the ships of Europe and the United States had changed it into a way station on the trade routes that crisscrossed the Pacific. The Tahiti of Gauguin's time was full of French soldiers and officials, English, American, and Chinese merchants, and native people who had given up their old religions and become Methodists and Catholics. It was a place with regular mail delivery, schools, and newspapers. All the things that were part of the modern world.

But Paul Gauguin, looking around at the place he'd come to, saw something different. The rich beauty of the island, with its red volcanic soil and deep brown beaches, its endless groves of coconut trees waving gracefully in the winds, the huge fleets of immense white clouds that came and went, and the vivid colors in everything, made it possible for him to imagine a world where ancient essences of truth and beauty still existed. This was what he painted, and he did it so well that a hundred years later it is this vision that most people think of when they think of Tahiti.

Gauguin lived in Tahiti twice; once for a few months in 1891, and again from 1892 to 1901. *Smoking Mirror* is set during this first visit. During this time, he painted many women, but only one man, a friend whom he called Totefa. Totefa appears five times in Gauguin's pictures from this period. The painting on the cover, called *Matamoe,* or *Peacocks in the Country,* is the last.

Each time Totefa appears, it marks a change in Gauguin's work. It is as if he is using his friend to announce that he has reached a new stage in his quest to unite the world around him with the one he was discovering inside himself. In Matamoe, he seems to be saying that he has succeeded. The traditional Tahitian house and the native figures in traditional clothing are combined with things from the outside world—the peafowl and the metal ax.

Who Totefa was, and why he was so important to Gauguin is as mysterious as the name Gauguin gave the painting. To this day, no one knows who Totefa really was, and the word *Matamoe* doesn't mean anything in any language Gauguin spoke. This mystery is at the heart of the Totefa paintings, and at the heart of this story.

Tahiti 1891

CHAPTER ONE

The *Artiste*

Tahiti was beautiful that afternoon. The sky was blue, the water inside the reef was turquoise, and the seagulls flying overhead were as white as flakes of the moon. The harbor was filling with canoes, more than I'd ever seen before. Big outriggers that could carry twenty people, small ones with one family aboard. Their sails were red and gold in the sunlight. I didn't really see any of it. I still couldn't believe Robert was dead.

A ship came in through the reef and joined the canoes. She was a little French navy gunboat, with a big flag flying from her mast and a cloud of white smoke rolling out of her funnel. It seemed as if the whole town of Papeete came running to the sound of her whistle.

The gunboat dropped anchor out in the harbor and lowered her longboat. Filled with passengers, it started toward the dock where I sat. Around me, the Tahitians were talking excitedly.

"The *Vire* is back. Who is aboard?"

"Why have they come?"

"Is the new marine captain here?"

It was just the same kind of talk Hawaiians did when a new ship came into Pearl Harbor. New people meant new stories, and there was nothing these island folks liked better than talking story with one another. Another time I might have joined in.

When the boat tied up, a couple ladies were handed up first. Then came a marine captain in his dress blues and a cork helmet as white as ice cream. Another officer, Lieutenant Jénot, got out behind him. I'd met him the day Robert was killed. He wouldn't be happy to see me, I guessed.

The Tahitians ahh'ed over the officers' braid and silver buttons. Then the last man in the boat got out.

At first I thought he might be a cowboy, because he was wearing a big, brand-new brown Stetson. But there was something about the way he lifted himself out of the boat that told me he was a sailor like myself.

He was a medium-sized fellow, strong-looking and wearing a mustache. His hair was brown and gray and flowed out from under his hat and down his back. He looked all around as if he were an explorer discovering something, took off his hat, then replaced it. I didn't have any idea to whom he was taking off his hat. He looked damned silly.

The Tahitians thought so too. They started smiling, then laughing as the fellow came toward me along the pier, talking French with the two officers. Everyone who'd come to see the gunboat was doing it. And others were coming to see what they were laughing at.

I knew why. I'd found out when I was living in Hawaii. The folks on those islands have some fellows called *mahús*. They dress and live like women. Nobody laughs at them; in fact, they're kind of sacred. But this guy with his long hair and his cowboy hat was like some kind of white *mahú*, and they thought maybe he was a clown, or maybe crazy.

I didn't feel like talking to anybody. But because of the hat, I thought maybe he was an American. And I reckoned he'd want to know why he was funny, so I said, "Hey, mister, you'd better get your hair cut if you're gonna stay in Tahiti. These folks all think think you're a lady."

He gave me a cold stare. I could tell he had understood my words, but he hadn't liked them.

I tried my French. "Your hair," I said. "They think your hair is feminine, but you dress like a man. That's why they laugh."

He looked me up and down as if there were something wrong with me.

"Imbecile," he drawled.

If Robert hadn't been dead, I'd have let it pass. But I was furious and I had to lash out. I swung my fist right into his face.

The next second I was lying flat on my back with the guy standing over me. He'd hit me three times to my one, and they'd felt like mule kicks.

"This is the sort of lady Paul Gauguin is, you ignorant pig," he said.

I started to get back up, but the marine officers pushed between us.

"Be off," Jénot said. "This man is an *artiste* and a goverment official, sent to paint the life of this colony. And as you can see, he is a better fighter than you. I warned you before, American. Leave Tahiti before worse things happen."

He gave me a shove that sent me back down on my haunches. I didn't dare take a poke at a marine lieutenant; I knew that. That'd be jail time for sure. And while I didn't care what happened to me in the long run, I had to stay free for right now. At least until I'd found Tehane, wherever she was on the island, and told her about Robert. Until the *Mateata* came back. Until I'd killed Gun, and maybe the White Wolf. Then I didn't care what happened. Which was good because, win or lose, Gun or the White Wolf would sure as sundown kill me.

So I just sat there while the artist and the marines walked on up the road toward the Cercle Militaire, the French officers' club. I didn't feel like laughing, but I did. I laughed at their backs as hard as I could. At that fake cowboy hat and the long hair hanging down under it.

CHAPTER TWO

Smoking Mirror

When I was little, back in Los Angeles, Abuelita used to tell me a lot about Old Mexico. Her family were Californios from way back, and she knew all the stories from the old country. She told me about La Llorona, the Weeping Woman, and that to see her face was death. She told me about the Aztecs and their gods, and the gods who'd been there before the Aztecs came. They were a mean bunch, those old gods. They drank the blood of warriors and sent it back to earth as rain.

The one I remember best was Smoking Mirror, Huitzilopchtli, whose name came from a shining black obsidian mirror in his forehead. He tricked the god of the Toltecs, Quetzalcoatl, out of his spot in heaven, and the Aztec gods took over. After that Smoking Mirror spent a lot of time lurking down on earth, looking for people to do things to. He was always looking for someone who had a good life and taking away whatever it was that had made it good, leaving the person ruined and in tears. I don't know why that story of all the others stuck with me. But I grew up thinking Smoking Mirror was still around, with nothing to do any more but watch me. It was like having a personal devil.

Once I asked, "Why is Smoking Mirror so mean, Abuelita? He's a god. He has everything he wants. Why does he have to take things away from people?"

At first she tried to tell me that Smoking Mirror didn't exist.

"Yes, he does," I said. "I can feel him at night."

Then she said my guardian angel would protect me from him. I didn't believe that.

Finally she sighed and said, "I was told when I was young that Smoking Mirror only tricks those who have been one way for too long. Everything must change, and Smoking Mirror is the changer. He destroys things, but something is left after. And sometimes what is left may be made better than what was before."

I believed that Abuelita believed that. But I still felt Smoking Mirror skulking at the edges of my life, like a coyote at the edge of a campfire.

He came close to me the first time when I was eight and Abuelita died. He came again when I was eleven and Mama went to join her.

That left me and Daddy alone on our little ranch outside Los Angeles. Daddy and I didn't get along too good. He was an Anglo from Texas, and Abuelita said he'd only married Mama to get her land. Once Mama was dead, I think it bothered him that I was still here. I don't think he liked my skin either. I was pretty brown. He seemed to think I'd let him down by not being whiter.

I always felt low around my dad. And now it was just the two of us.

Some days he didn't talk to me at all. Then there were the days when he did.

"Why the hell can't you keep that fence mended?" he asked, before I knew there was anything wrong with one of our fences. "It ain't hard to tack up bobwire to a post." Or "You trimmed my horse's hoofs like you used a crosscut saw. You know better'n that. Now go do it right." And I'd do the same job I'd done before, and he'd go on to something else. But he saved his meanest words for special occasions: "You did that like a Mexican. Fix it white."

That went on for a few years until Smoking Mirror passed by again and we lost the ranch to the Southern Pacific Railroad. Daddy took a look at the foreclosed signs on the fences, took a look at me, and said, "Guess I'll go into town."

He left me standing there on the road, and that was the last I saw of him. I was fourteen.

Well, that was it. I knew now I was no good to anybody. I felt as if I didn't belong on the earth. So when I was sure he was gone and not coming back, I got off the earth as much as I could. I went down to San Pedro and hired myself out on the first ship that would take me.

That had been two years ago and almost ten thousand miles away. Now it seemed as if Smoking Mirror had found me again.

Two days ago this time, Robert had been alive, and we'd been shipmates. Now he was lying on a slab at the police station with three bullets in him, and the one who'd done it was somewhere over the horizon.

I'd met Robert Fort in Pearl Harbor, where his ship had docked on her run from Australia. She was American, but he was a French-man—from Normandy, like almost all French sailors—and he was looking for a new berth. Robert was older than I was, about nineteen to my fifteen, and a hell of a lot smarter and more educated. I didn't know any French then; but he knew some English, and he knew Tahitian and I knew Hawaiian, which is almost the same. We hit it right off.

Robert was the kind of friend I'd wanted all my life. He was like a hero in a book—not that I'd read that many books; but the ones I had read all had heroes in them who were handsome and brave and honest, and that was Robert, right down to the keel. And he liked me. I didn't know why, but I didn't much care. All I wanted was to be shipmates with him forever.

I'd been hanging out in Waikiki, learning to talk Hawaiian and how to surf. But Robert had to get back to Tahiti, where Tehane was. We agreed to ship out together, and we found a five-master named *The Princess of Hilo* that was going there on her way to New Zealand. We signed on.

How Robert'd ever got tangled up with the White Wolf I never knew. That was before my time. But two days ago, when we'd been walking down by Papeete Harbor with our seabags on our backs, he'd looked out over the water and seen a good-sized, dirty sloop rid-ing at anchor.

"Joe, that is the *Mateata*. The worst hell-ship I was ever on. There are men aboard her I don't want to see. Let's get away from this place."

It was the first time I'd ever seen him scared.

"*Très bien,*" I'd said. "But where do we go?"

Papeete was small, and there weren't many places to hide.

Robert thought for a minute and said, "The cathedral."

The cathedral was as far away from the waterfront as you could get and still be in town. We started up the street that led that way.

"Now, *mon copain,* what is this?" I asked.

"I jumped ship off the *Mateata* here in Papeete a few years ago. When I did, I killed a man. A big Hawaiian named Keoki. His mate Gun will be looking for me if he's still alive. And so will the White Wolf. It's the worst damned luck, him being in port when we are."

"But wait a minute," I said. "Even if these fellows do want to kill you, they wouldn't dare do it in Papeete would they?"

"Gun will do anything he wants to," Robert said. "He's mad."

We hurried on toward the cathedral.

"This fellow Gun is a giant," Robert said. "From the Marquesas Islands, I think. Covered with tribal tattoos. He has a bright red beard, like a lot of Marquesans. And he always carries a pair of pistols. Often a rifle."

"Why did you kill the Hawaiian?" I asked.

"He tried to stop me from leaving," Robert said. "Then I went over the side and swam to shore. That was here. That was when I met Tehane."

Tehane and Robert had fallen in love two years before. She'd been too young to get married then. She'd be just old enough now, and Robert had come back to see if she still loved him.

That was all I knew about her.

We hurried on past the Cercle Militaire.

As we passed it, we heard a voice.

"*Arrêtez*, Fort, *arrêtez!*"

We turned around, and there, just a few yards behind us, were a tall, silver-haired Frenchman and Gun. It had to be him. There couldn't be two men in the world who looked like that. And damned if Gun didn't have a small black tattoo in the middle of his forehead, the ace of spades. He was like a nightmare gone walking.

For a second everyone froze.

"I am unarmed," Robert shouted.

But Gun just dropped the bundle he had been carrying, pulled out two long-barreled Colts, and ran toward Robert, roaring some words I couldn't understand. When Gun was just beyond arm's reach, he fired: two shots from one of the pistols, one shot from the other.

I saw the life go out of my friend's face. I really think he was dead before he hit the ground.

The giant, or monster or whatever he was ran on down toward the harbor. But the tall Frenchman walked over to where I was kneeling by Robert and pushed at him with his boot.

"One way or another, everyone pays what he owes me," he said.

Women were screaming, men were shouting, and I was begging, "Oh, Robert, don't die. Get up. Come on, get up now; let's go find Tehane." I don't remember everything I said. How could I?

His hand was limp and heavy as lead.

In a minute the *gendarmes* were there in their uniforms and helmets.

"What has happened here?" one of them said.

"A man shot my friend" was all I could say. "A big man with tattoos. He ran down toward the harbor. Go get him."

But around me several voices said, "He was with the White Wolf."

"The White Wolf?" said one of the *gendarmes.* "Did anyone see him here?"

"*Oui,* I did," I said. "He went—"

There was no sign of him.

"Well, I'll bet he's gone back to his ship. The *Mateata,*" I said. "If you run, you can catch him."

"First things first," one of the *gendarmes* said. "This man must be dealt with. You must come along with us."

"But he's getting away!" I shouted.

"When we have your report, we will see what needs to be done," the other *gendarme* said.

The first *gendarme* ordered a couple of men to pick up Robert's body.

"Wait! I can't. I'll come back," I said. And I started to run.

I got about one step before one of the *gendarmes* reached out and clubbed me. I sprawled in the dirt.

"Justice is a slow process but a fair one," the *gendarme* said, yanking me up. "We require your information. Come with us."

I was taller than the *gendarme,* but we both knew who the big man was. I followed along behind Robert with the *gendarme's* hand tight on my arm.

When we got to the police station, I told the whole story. Then I told it again. And again. Then the *gendarmes* asked me a bunch of questions about who would pay for the funeral and who Robert's family were.

I knew he had a mother in Normandy. He wrote to her and sent money sometimes. But there was nothing in his pockets with her address.

"Tehane might know," I said. "If you help me find her, maybe she'll have it."

"This Tehane," one of the *gendarmes* said. "What is her surname? Does she live here in Papeete?"

"I don't know," I said.

The *gendarme* shrugged. "It is a pity. The name is common. And she could be anywhere on the island. Where did he meet her? Behind the Cercle Militaire?"

"No, sir," I said. I'd only been in Papeete a couple of days, but I'd seen the kinds of things that went on behind the Cercle Militaire and the kind of girls who went there. Robert wouldn't have come back to marry one of them.

"Then we have no clues," the *gendarme* said.

"He has money," said another *gendarme* coming in from where Robert's body lay. "He can pay for his burial."

"Then we may conclude this matter," said the one who'd been asking me questions.

"But what are you going to do about it?" I said.

"We shall keep your evidence; and when the *Mateata* returns, we shall inquire to see if anyone matching your colorful description of the supposed murderer is aboard her," said the *gendarme*.

"You mean she's gone? You let her get away?" I couldn't believe it. They'd kept me sitting here while the *Mateata* had sailed.

"It is of no great importance," said the gendarme. "The *Mateata* is often in the harbor. She will return sooner or later. In any case, we had no reason to detain a simple copra trader heading out for another cargo. As for you, you may go."

The *gendarme* who'd hit me took me by the arm again and marched me out. On the way he practically bumped me into that marine officer who'd shoved me this morning.

"Pardon, Lieutenant Jénot," the *gendarme* said, and finished getting me out of the building.

Once I was in the street, I just stood there. I didn't have an idea what to do next. Finally my feet started to move, and I just went wherever they carried me. I couldn't think. All I knew was that Robert was dead, his killer was loose, and I was alone.

Hours later, I was walking down by the harbor again when I saw that Lieutenant Jénot. He saw me too and hurried over.

"I'm sorry about your friend, sailor," he said.

"What's it to you?" I asked.

"Nothing, as it turns out," he answered. "When I heard of the murder and who had committed it, I went to police headquarters to learn more. The White Wolf is involved in many things, some of which are not only illegal but may be dangerous to France in these islands. Those are the ones in which I take an interest. But your friend's death does not seem to have been one of these. Therefore, I am sorry he is dead."

"Your damned *gendarmes* let him get away," I said. "Can you do anything about it?"

"Your friend will not receive justice," Jénot said. "I wish it were not true, but it is. The White Wolf is a rogue and everyone knows it. But he is well connected here in Papeete. The governor and others protect him to a certain extent. If his thug Gun shoots a seaman now and again, it will not matter much."

"They wouldn't even let me go after him," I said. "They hit me from behind."

"They did you a favor," Jénot said. "If you'd caught up to the White Wolf and that beast he keeps, you'd have been killed too. Now go. And take my advice and find another ship. Never come back to Tahiti."

CHAPTER THREE

Titi

I reckon that marine thought he was giving me friendly advice. But he didn't know me, and he didn't know Robert. Robert deserved better than that. I would see that he got it.

The problem with that was, I didn't have a weapon. Nothing. I had a hatchet and a good knife, but that didn't count. Not against someone like Gun. Even that artist had decked me, and he wasn't more than half the size of Gun. I needed an equalizer, something about forty-five caliber.

I had a few dollars in pay, but probably not enough to buy a six-gun. Tahiti was expensive. And I needed money to live on while I went looking for Tehane.

All this was what I had been running my mind on there on the dock.

The people who'd come to watch the gunboat arrive were starting to wander away home. It was time for siesta. Everything in Papeete would close up until about four. Before long it was just me and the gulls there on the dock.

I couldn't help it. I cried for Robert. Then I cried for myself. I even found some tears for Tehane, whoever she was.

I started to wander. Finally I ended up in front of the little cathedral. The doors were open, but I didn't go in. If we could have made it here two days ago, Robert would still be alive. I felt as if God had let us down. God was in there, I knew—Abuelita's God, and Mama's. His light was burning in the candle flame by the altar. His body, in bread, was in the tabernacle. I didn't want to see Him.

He hadn't protected Robert from Smoking Mirror.

There were some graves beside the church. One of them had a statue of a sad-faced woman on top of a stone column. I leaned against that column and sank down and cried some more. And then, when I was dry of tears, the damnedest thing happened. I fell asleep.

The thought of Robert came over me again, and I had to get away from that place. I wanted to go and visit his grave, but I realized I didn't even know where it was. He might not even be buried yet. I started walking aimlessly again.

But something stopped me before I'd gone far. It was a crowd of people gathered in front of a big stone building almost as high as the cathedral. It had a fence around it, gardens, and iron gates. It looked as different from the flowery little palm-thatched houses with their steep, high roofs, or the wooden storefronts and hotels as if it had been dropped from the sky. I'd passed it a dozen times or more since Robert had been shot, but now the gates were locked and two marines stood behind them with bayonets on their rifles.

I wondered what they were on guard against. Not the crowd, it seemed. They were just standing in front of the gates, silent and watching. There were sailors like me, or Chinese, or businessmen with no business to tend to. But most of the people were Tahitians, standing quietly, watching the building.

The feel of waiting drew me. I decided the police station could be put off for a little while. I joined the crowd.

"Reckon they'll drop a handkerchief?" I heard one fellow say.

"Oh, sure," his friend replied. "They know what's right to do. Just because they're natives don't mean they can't act civilized when they want to."

A white handkerchief dropped from an upstairs window would mean someone was dead. Everybody knew that. Who? I wondered. But no handkerchief dropped. The only cloth to see was a red-and-white flag flapping in the afternoon wind. It made a lonely sound.

After a while I felt someone take my hand. I turned and looked into the face of a woman a few years older than I was and a couple of inches taller.

"You American?" she asked quietly.

"Yeah," I said.

"I like Americans," she said. "You a sailor?"

"Yep."

"I like sailors. It's hot. Take me for a drink. My name's Titi," she said.

I didn't feel like having a drink with this girl, but I thought maybe she could help me find Tehane. I sure didn't know anyone else to ask. And I knew her kind well enough to know she'd expect to be paid for any help she gave me. A drink or two would be little enough.

"Come on," she said. "The king won't die until tomorrow morning. Get me a drink."

She practically pulled me away from the gate.

"What king?" I asked as we walked away. "I didn't know this place had a king."

"Oh, it has a king," she smirked. "A little king. A drunk. Pomare V. He's drunk all the time. I hear he drinks himself to death so he won't have to see any more Frenchmen. And when he dies, France takes over."

She shrugged.

"I thought France already owned Tahiti," I said.

"Everything but the king," Titi said.

I thought of the canoes filling the harbor. Suddenly it struck me as strange.

"Titi, how do these people know it's time?" I said. "Who told them?"

"Oh, the sun told them," she said. "Some of these little islands, they have places on their mountains that turn black at sunset when a king or queen is going to die."

Black spots on the mountains that told the deaths of kings. Well, I'd learned of stranger things in Hawaii, such as the ghosts that come down from the mountains on Kaui when one of the Hawaiian kings dies. How could I doubt the truth of what she said? The proof was in the harbor.

"How do you know the king won't die until tomorrow?" I said.

"He'll die when the tide goes out," Titi said. "They always do. All the kings and queens. What's your name?"

"Joe Sloan," I said.

"It's nice you're an American. I'm half English. That's why I speak such good English," Titi said. "I do, don't I?"

"Good enough," I said.

"I'm half English, the queen's half English. It's good to be half something and half something, don't you think so? What are you?"

"Half Anglo, half Mexican," I said.

"So you're like me; that's good," Titi said. "I can talk English, French and Tahitian. What can you talk?"

"English and Spanish, French, and Hawaiian," I said. "And Tahitian."

"That's a lot. You must be smart," Titi said.

"I grew up with Spanish and English," I said. "If you know those, French is easy. And Hawaiian and Tahitian are a lot alike. It wasn't so hard."

"That's because you're smart," Titi said. "Pretty, too. Do you think I'm pretty?"

I wasn't in the mood for this kind of chat, but there was nothing I could do about it except let her run on, saying whatever came into her head. Finally we came to a place that was open and sold beer and soda water. Titi had the one and I had the other. I had a good idea that Titi wanted to get drunk, and that wasn't part of my plan for myself right then.

Titi went on and on, talking about herself and how nice I was. I wasn't listening. I was thinking about Pomare dying, and a whole nation dying with him. It reminded me of what had happened to my mother's people, the Verdugos. They'd once owned a *rancho* you needed a day to ride across. Then the *gringos* came, and by the time I was born all the Verdugos had was the house we lived in and sixty acres. I felt bad about that, even though I was half *gringo* myself. Now we'd lost that.

On the second or third beer, I decided I'd been nice enough and asked her if she knew a girl named Tehane.

She squinted at me.

"What do you want to talk about another girl for?"

"Never mind why," I said. "Just tell me. Do you know a girl named Tehane? Maybe part French?"

"No," she said, and swigged her beer.

"Titi, I like you," I lied. "I just need to find this girl for—for a friend. If he wanted to find her, how would he do it?"

Titi shrugged.

"Just look around," she said. "Ask all the girls. They're all here right now. For the funeral. Just ask."

It drove me near crazy to think that Tehane might be here, probably was here, and that I might walk past her at any minute. Think, I told myself. Didn't Robert ever tell you anything about Tehane except that she was wonderful?

No. He never did.

"I've got to get going," I said to Titi. "I need to find Tehane."

"I hope she is fat and ugly," Titi said.

"She won't be," I said. "See you around, Titi."

Titi didn't answer.

By now it was full dark. Not the best time for searching, but I looked into the face of every woman's who passed; and if she looked as if she might be the right age, I said the name "Tehane." All I got were some surprised looks back.

Finally, a long time past midnight, I went back to the palace. It was dark except for a couple of low lights up on the second floor.

The crowd at the gates all seemed to be Tahitian now. It was a warm night, but the people stood as close to one another as if they'd been knotted. Broad-backed men and proud-standing women with babies on their shoulders, all talking quietly and watching those lights.

I looked up at the sky, and the stars seemed to be extra low and bright. I had the feeling they were with the Tahitians, waiting and watching.

I watched with them; and while I watched, the wind died. The fat clouds slowed and stopped, and hung above us. The cocoa palms stopped swaying and rustling.

From somewhere on the other side of the crowd came a deep voice, a woman's, singing a sad song. The song spread, and in a minute everyone was singing it. They broke it into parts, everyone sailing into his or her own places. I recognized the tune. I'd heard it in seamen's missions and at Sunday services aboard ship. It was "Nearer, My God, to Thee."

> *Though like the wanderer the sun gone down*
> *Darkness be over me, my rest a stone.*
> *Yet in my dreams I'll be nearer, my God, to thee.*

The wind came back as if they'd called it with their song. Maybe they had. The palms began to move again, and the clouds went on their way to wherever they were heading.

In the silver shadows on the palace balcony, someone moved. A piece of cloth white as the moonlight drifted to the ground.

There was a rustling in the crowd as the women took their white tiare flowers out from behind their ears—right ears if they were married, left ears if they weren't—and let them drop.

The king was dead. But the Tahitians had already known that. The wind had told them. That was why they'd started singing. They went on with their song and began a new one. I walked away. I'd done all I could for now and taken all I could take.

I walked down toward the beach, feeling sorrow rise in me again.

It was the turn of the tide.

CHAPTER FOUR

A Hat from Buffalo Bill

When I finally slept, it was between the tombs by the cathedral. It kept me out of the wind.

The next day I washed my face in a little stone birdbath and went looking for something to eat.

Most of the stores had black crepe on their doors now, and the flagpole at the palace was already flying the French tricolor at half-mast. They hadn't wasted any time raising it.

I found a place in the Chinese market where I could get hot rice and a couple of sticky buns cheap, and washed them down with a cup of coffee.

Once I'd eaten I felt better. Not good, but strong enough to do what needed doing. I started my search for Tehane again.

As I wandered around, I picked up some of the news. The king's funeral would be held off for three days. That would give folks from the islands who didn't have black spots time to get the news and come in to Papeete.

The town got fuller throughout the day. Nobody expected any

trouble from the natives, it was said; but I noticed more patrols of
French marines on the streets than I'd seen the day before. They
marched past in squads, wearing their fancy blue jackets and their
big, white cork helmets with bayonets shining above them. They
didn't seem to be going anywhere in particular. They were just
reminding everyone who was in charge.

I kept up a patrol of my own, walking through the streets looking
into women's faces. Whenever I saw someone about the right age, I
asked if her name was Tehane. Three or four times it was, but it was
never the right one.

I had the same fool-sounding conversation each time.

"Excuse me, are you named Tehane?"

"Yes."

"Are you in love with Robert Fort?"

"No."

"Excuse me, but do you know any other girl named Tehane?
About your age?"

"No."

By the end of the second day, the Tahitians had given me a name.
I was Tehane Man. I didn't mind it. I hoped maybe the real Tehane
would hear of me and come to find out what I wanted. But that
didn't happen.

A couple of times I saw Titi, who ignored me. She was at the
Cercle Militaire on the arm of that artist, Gauguin. He was sitting
between her and those marine officers who'd gotten off the boat
with him. He had a lei of orchids around his neck and was still
wearing his cowboy hat. His hair was still long too. He looked more

ridiculous than ever, but he seemed mighty satisfied with himself.

When he wasn't with Titi, Gauguin was out on the streets with a big pad of paper and a pencil. He was sketching people's faces. He'd wait until they weren't looking, then start drawing. After they'd moved on, he kept on, I guess until he was satisfied. Then he'd start sneaking up—that's what it seemed like to me—on someone else.

I didn't think much of a man who would make pictures of people without their say-so. But what really got under my blanket was the look on his face, the look he'd had sitting next to Titi. He looked as if he thought he owned Tahiti and everything on it. The cock of his head and the light in those heavy-lidded eyes were more than I could stand.

What does it matter? I told myself. He's nothing to you, and you're nothing to him. Get on with what you have to do and let him go to hell his own way.

But every time I saw him, the feeling that I wanted to take another poke at that stupid, smug face got stronger.

The third day came and went. By now I looked pretty ratty in spite of my tries at washing up. Living outside shows on you, no matter what you do. But with a funeral to go to, I hauled my last clean shirt and britches out of my seabag and put them on. I bought a black rosette to wear on my chest and a black band for my arm, and I joined the procession to Pomare's tomb.

I have to say, the French did right by him that day. The marines followed his hearse with their flag dipped low, marching slowly in time with the band playing the "Dead March" over and over.

Then came the French officials and the rich people in their carriages, throwing up a big cloud of coral dust from the road. The dust settled out on the Tahitians coming behind in their clans, every clan following its own brand-new French flag.

Bringing up the rear came the people like me. People without any money or clan, or any flag to follow, or any reason to be there. Unless they had some personal cause to follow Pomare down to the beach to his grave.

The sun got hotter and hotter as we walked, and the dust settled more and more thickly on our eyes and in our mouths. I began to get real tired of that death march.

I didn't really feel sorry for the king. He'd drunk himself to death, that was all. I did feel sorry for the Tahitians, though I couldn't see that they'd be worse off without him than with him. So why was I there?

Partly I was doing it because I thought it was the right thing to do. Not to have come would have been disrespectful, and I had no reason to be that. Mostly I was marching for Robert, trying to give him a little of the funeral he deserved.

Okay, King Pomare, I thought. You've drunk your last drink and played your last card. You weren't much of a king, I guess, but maybe you did the best you could. My friend Robert is here too. Share some of this with him. He deserved it better than you did. And for that matter, here's Joe Sloan with his own death mark on him and a gunfight to die in, thanks to Smoking Mirror. Likely this is all the funeral I'll ever get. So share a little with me too, and I'll follow you to your burying.

Finally we reached the place on the beach where Pomare had built his tomb. It was a big pile of coral blocks painted red, and it said POMARE in black letters over the door.

The governor got up and made a long speech. It went on a lot longer than the words used to bury Pomare that some minister spoke afterward.

With the sun frying my brain, I gave up even trying to pay attention to all that talking and started looking around me. A way off from me, I saw Gauguin, sketching again. And he was still wearing his hat.

A surge of anger big as a breaker wave rose up inside me. That damn artist had no business drawing pictures now, and no right to wear a hat at a funeral.

I started to ease my way through the crowd until I was standing behind him. Then I ripped the hat from his head and threw it on the ground.

Gauguin whipped around. At first he looked surprised. Then he recognized me and curled his lip.

"*Tabu*," I hissed. "*Tabu*." That's Tahitian for "forbidden," and why I used that word I don't know. It just came to me.

Gauguin's face changed again. Those heavy-lidded eyes lost their anger, and his lip uncurled. He cocked his head in that way he had and gave me a sort of nod.

Somehow that made it okay for me to bend over and pick up his hat. Gauguin took it, put it under his arm, and closed his sketchpad. Then he turned away from me, and I moved off.

When the business of the funeral was finally over, we started back for town. The carriages dashed on ahead. The marines moved off at a quick march and left the rest of us behind. With no Frenchmen there to see them, the Tahitians let their flags droop and drag in the dust.

The people weren't drooping though. As soon as the French were gone, they started chatting with one another as happy as birds. They talked about the funeral, about how nice the marines had looked, and wasn't that a good long speech? They talked about the trim on the tomb, how bright it was, and what to have for dinner. They talked about whether to go dancing or singing that night and about going home.

Well, I thought, if this were my funeral, I'm satisfied with it. Robert would have liked it, too.

Then, as I walked along wondering what to do next, I heard the words, "Come on, Tehane, there are tiares over there."

And I saw her.

It had to be her. Even though I was looking at her from behind, I knew that if this wasn't the Tehane I'd been looking for, I'd never find her. She was wearing a long, black dress that the dust had turned brown; and her hair, blacker than the dress, fell down her back. Her arms were creamy gold, and I was sure her face was beautiful.

She was standing in the middle of a clutch of women and girls—cousins, sisters, and aunts, I figured—and they were part of a lot more women who all broke their walk to go over to the roadside to pull the big, white tiare flowers off the bushes and twine them in their hair.

I watched closely while Tehane did hers. It went behind her left ear. She had waited for Robert. So I believed. Who wouldn't wait for him? Anyway, she was unmarried for sure.

It crossed my mind for just a second that maybe this wasn't her after all. But when I saw that face, I knew it had to be. This girl was good enough for Robert.

I felt like—I don't know how I felt. Lighter, excited, and afraid of what I was going to have to do all at once. I wanted to run over to her and blurt out who I was and why I was there, and then—then get on with the other thing. But this was no place to tell her what I had to say. No place to tell her her sweetheart was dead.

I'd just have to be sure not to lose her. Soon enough, when this crowd was all back in town and broken up, I could do that.

So I followed along behind, as close as was decent, keeping my eyes on her. But then, a little farther on, she and the other women did something I couldn't watch. The road passed a wide, shallow stream in one place, and they all waded into it to cool off their legs, hiking up their skirts.

I hurried on down the road to wait for Tehane to pass. I sat there while the other men went by; and in a while I saw Gauguin again, walking along on the other side of the road. We nodded. Then, to my surprise, he crossed the road to me.

"You have been a sailor," he said to me in French.

"I am a sailor," I said.

"So am I," Gauguin said.

"I could tell," I said. "You walk like one."

"You did well today," he said. "That is why I did not strike you as I did the first time. Your anger was the just anger of a warrior. I too am a warrior. Do you know of the American cowboy Buffalo Bill?"

Didn't everybody? Buffalo Bill's Wild West Show Featuring Riders of All Nations was probably the best-known circus in the whole world. My daddy had even met Bill Cody once, when he tried out for a job with his outfit. He always said Bill Cody was the biggest windbag in the United States, including the president and both houses of Congress.

But Gauguin was taking off his hat and handing it to me.

"I visited the Wild West Show of Buffalo Bill in Paris just before I came to Tahiti," he said. "I bought this hat there. I do not think it suits me. I offer it to you."

A few days ago we'd taken punches at each other. Now he was giving me his hat. And it was a beauty. I'd never had such a hat back in Los Angeles. I put it on. It fit well, though I could see I was going to have to knock the brim into something less dudish when I got the chance.

"A thousand thanks," I said.

"One warrior to another," he said, and went on his way.

What was this warrior stuff? I wondered. He sounded as if he thought we were both Indians. But it didn't matter. The hat mattered. I hadn't had one like it since I'd gone to sea. Since Daddy'd lost the ranch to the railroad company. That hat somehow connected me to my old good times, such as they were, when Mama and Daddy and Abuelita and I had all been a family.

As I sat there studying the gift I'd been given, Tehane walked by with her family.

I got up and followed when they were a little way ahead.

Things didn't go the way I'd planned when we got back to

Papeete. Tehane's family went in separate directions. Some went to find parties. Others headed down to the docks; Tehane was with them. At the water, there was a big crowd of people getting into their outriggers. All of a sudden there was a wall of Tahitians between me and her, and by the time I pushed through it, she was in one of the outriggers, paddling out toward the reef.

"Tehane, Tehane, where are you going?" I shouted, but she didn't hear me.

Well, I wasn't going to lose her again, I decided. I jumped into the harbor and swam after her. But that didn't work. There were four big men with paddles in that outrigger, and they had a sail. They pulled away from me fast.

Just to make it perfect, when I got back to the docks, practically too tired to stand, there was Titi.

"Is that the girl you wanted?" she said. "She doesn't seem to want you."

"Go haunt a house," I said.

"That girl probably lives on some little island a hundred miles away," Titi said. "She's probably never been to Papeete before, and I bet she never comes again."

But someone else was on the dock right then. One of the women who'd been with Tehane.

In my Hawaiian Tahitian I asked her, "Where is that canoe going? Can you tell me?"

"That depends on why you want to know," she said.

"I have a . . . story . . . for someone on it. It's bad news. Big news. Please tell me."

She looked me up and down. My rosette had come off, and my armband was around my wrist now.

"You were at the funeral," she said.

"Yes," I said.

"That was good," the woman said. "I think you are probably good too. I will tell you where the canoe comes from. Do you know where Mataiea is?"

I shook my head.

"Up the coast about a day's walk from here. Go that way."

She pointed to the south.

"Mataiea. Thank you," I said.

Then I looked around and saw Titi was still close by.

"Hey, Titi," I called. "She lives in Mataiea."

"She would," Titi called back. "It's as boring and ugly as she is."

CHAPTER FIVE

Tehane

I went to Robert's grave the next day. It was a little hill of fresh red earth with a blank white stone the size of a skull.

"I found Tehane, Robert," I said. "Don't get too far ahead, *mon copain*. I'll be with you soon."

I was off for Mataiea as soon as I'd eaten and bought a little food for my trip.

Any other time I think I'd have believed I'd died and gone to heaven, walking along that road. For one thing, there was food for the taking, just like in the Garden of Eden. Breadfruit and red bananas grew everywhere, and coconuts lay on the ground, just waiting to be split open. I hadn't needed to buy a thing in Papeete.

The road ran through a wide plain that reached all the way to Aori, the volcano that towered over everything on Tahiti. I walked through miles of country thick with chestnut trees and cocoa palms and bananas. There were little farms and villages too, and people ready to talk story with anyone who passed. There were broad brown beaches, and turquoise water ran out to the reef. Out beyond the reef, the water was dark and the waves flew up against the coral like white horses rearing.

Plenty of real horses passed me too. Tahitians loved to ride. And there were a couple of mail coaches with passengers making the trip to Mataiea and back. If I could have afforded a ticket, I'd have been there in a couple of hours.

But I was in no hurry. Now that I knew who Tehane was, and where to find her, I had to think about just what I was going to tell her. I wanted some time to work on that in my mind. One day more or less wouldn't make much difference. Besides, when I had told her, it would be time to get serious about finding a gun, and getting ready to use it.

The other thing that slowed me up was the *maraes*. I couldn't pass one without stopping.

Robert had told me about them, but I hadn't had a clear notion of what he'd meant until I saw my first one. It was a tower of stones taller than the trees shaped like a pyramid with steps made of black rock. When I went closer, I saw it had a sort of field in front of it marked off with boulders and big enough for a fair-sized cattle pen.

Robert had told me every clan had its own, and the men used to gather there to worship the gods. There were big *maraes* and small *maraes*, all abandoned now. Most of the clans that built them had died out in the plagues the sailors brought, and those that were left were all church people, so they didn't have any use for them.

I climbed to the top of that first one, just to see how far I could see; but the trees were tall enough so that the only direction in which I could look any distance was out over the reef; and there was nothing out that way but another island called Moorea, and beyond that a lot of water.

It was a sad place. It felt empty, and I knew it would stay empty forever. Maybe somebody else would have said he or she could almost hear the old voices or feel the spirits of the dead. But all I touched was the loneliness of the stones.

After that I didn't climb any more of them, but I always stopped and looked a good long time when I passed one, wondering who had built it and what they'd been like. The old Mexicans had done the same back before the Spaniards came. Built huge pyramids and cut open warriors on top of them to pull out their hearts and give them to gods such as Smoking Mirror.

I wondered how people as far apart as Mexico and Tahiti and even Old Egypt had come up with the same idea, and why. The Tahitians didn't build anything else big, or anything else out of stone. Shoot, their houses were half falling down as often as not. What had mattered so much?

Thinking and looking, it took me two days to get to Mataiea.

When I walked into town it was night, and the breeze was off the ocean, making the palms dance. As I passed the first houses, I heard a new sound joining the thud of the waves and the soft creak of the trees. It was a loud, strong sound coming from up ahead where a big fire glowed.

I walked past a white-painted store with signs on it in French, English, and Chinese, and a little jail made out of pink coral. There were some schools and churches. Mataiea looked to be a pretty big place, for Tahiti.

As I got closer to the fire, I recognized what the people were singing. It was a hymn, one I knew from Abuelita. I reckoned these folks must be Catholics.

Not having anything else to do, I went over and stood at the edge of the firelight. When they finished that song, they went on to another, one I didn't know, so I just listened. They sure were good, loud singers. The men sang low like the sea outside the reef, and the women sang high like the wind in the trees. The sound had kind of a rough edge to it that I liked. When they started another song I knew, I joined in, singing the Spanish words.

Then we did another that I knew, and darned if it didn't make me feel a little better to be singing it. My pain was dulled a little by the music. I sat down at the edge of the firelight and joined in on every song I could recognize.

After a while a man looked over at me and smiled and stretched out his hand. He was a big Tahitian with some gray in his hair and a soft smile.

I came on over and sat beside him.

"*Ia orana,*" he said. "You are new."

"*Ia orana,*" I said. "Yes. I just got here."

"It is good the first thing you did was come to the *himene*. You like to sing?"

"It makes me feel better," I said. "Call me Anani," the man said. "You know what *Anani* means? It means 'orange.' I grow oranges."

"I'm Joe Sloan," I said.

"English?"

"No, American," I said.

Then the song leader gave us the first line of a new one, and the voices rose all around me like glad thunder.

It was late when the singing ended. People picked up and started heading for their homes.

"Come with us, Totefa," Anani said to me. "Sleep at my place."

Totefa. I smiled when he called me that. *Totefa* was "Joseph," reworked into Tahitian. If he'd given me a Tahitian name, he must like me.

Anani had a huge family, who all found sleeping places in a brand-new two-story Sears & Roebuck house imported from the States. I slung my hammock in a room with a couple of his sons. The windows were open and the breeze blew through all night. I slept hard, but before dawn I woke up in a sweat, thinking about Robert.

"What is the matter?" one of Anani's boys asked me. He was a kid about eleven years old named Anapa. "You said things in your sleep."

"Bad dreams," I said. "Sorry."

"Bad dreams? Bad dreams about what?" he asked.

"Sorry," I said again. And pretended to go back to sleep.

The next day at breakfast, Anani asked me why I had come to Mataiea. I told him about Robert and Tehane and the White Wolf, and Gun. I didn't mention that I was planning to kill anybody. It didn't seem smart.

"Tehane de Pouning," said Mrs. Anani, whose first name was Tehura. "That little half-French girl who likes to read so much. She lives with her mother over by the Catholic school. You must have passed her house last night."

"I remember your friend," Anani said. "When he was here, he

helped me with my trees sometimes. If you are going to stay here, maybe you would like to help me. I will give you a place to live and two francs each day you work."

"Let me see how it goes with Miss Tehane," I said, and stood up from the table. "Can I leave my seabag here until I know if I'm staying?"

"Of course," Anani said.

My feet felt as if they had lead weights on them as I walked over to Tehane's place. The good feelings of the *himene* were gone as if they'd never been.

Tehane's house was a big old place with a high, thatched roof and walls made out of logs that let the wind blow through. It sat under a couple of chestnut trees and had a garden and a little fence. A red dog lay beside the front door with his eyes mostly closed. He gave me one soft *wuf* to let me know he was on the job.

I went up and knocked.

A tall, dark woman answered it. I could see a little of the girl I'd come for in her face.

"*Ia orana*," I said. "My name is Totefa Asalona," I said, giving my name in Tahitian. "I have a message for Mademoiselle Tehane."

"*Ia orana*" she said. "Is it from Robert Fort?"

"*Oui, madame.* It is about Robert Fort," I said.

"Come in."

I stood in the big, cool front room and waited. I heard the woman's voice and the girl's. Soon a curtain lifted and Tehane came through it.

She was wearing a beautiful blue-and-white dress, with her tiare

behind her ear and a crystal necklace around her neck. It was as if she
had dressed to meet her sweetheart.

"You have news for me of Robert?" she asked me in French. She
was smiling like the sun on the water.

"*Oui*," I answered.

"Sit down, please," she said.

"Could we talk outside?" I asked.

Her face changed.

"It is bad, isn't it?" she said.

"As bad as it can be," I told her. "*Mademoiselle*—your—our
friend is dead."

First Tehane stared at me. Then her eyes filled with tears and she
dropped down and leaned against the wall.

"How?" she asked at last.

"Shot in Papeete," I said. "A Marquesan named Gun. He sailed
away with the White Wolf. But don't you worry, *mademoiselle*," I
said. "I'll get them for it."

Then she really started to cry. Her mother came back and took
her in her arms, and she cried too.

I didn't know what to do, so I went outside and listened to the
weeping coming from the house, and waited. I thought maybe they'd
want to know more, or there'd be something I could do for them.
And anyway, I didn't have anyplace else to go.

It was a long time before anyone came back to the door.

Finally the older woman came and invited me in, in Tahitian.

Tehane was sitting on an old wicker couch. Her face was pale and
her throat was wet where the tears had run.

"You have come a long way to bring us this news. We should welcome you," the woman said. "I am Maria, Tehane's mother."

I nodded.

"Tell me how you knew Robert," Tehane said. Her voice was trembly.

I sat down, and I told them all I could. And once I started talking, it was as if I couldn't stop. Every story I remembered recalled another one to me, and I told them all, important or not. If my words had been tears, I'd have drowned us all.

It was afternoon by the time I'd finished talking.

"You loved him too," Tehane said.

"He was my best pal," I said using the English word.

"You loved him," Tehane said. "Stay with us awhile. Help me mourn. Please."

"I'll do whatever you want," I said.

Tehane stood up. She wasn't real steady on her feet.

"I must go to pray for him in the church," she said. "Will you go with us?"

I couldn't go into a church. I was still too angry at God.

"I'll go with you as far as the door," I said.

No one said anything to that.

We all went off to church, Tehane walking between her mother and me for support. Most of the time she held herself as straight as a mast, but once or twice she stumbled a little and we caught her.

The old dog trailed along behind with his head low and his tail down. Maybe he'd loved Robert too.

It seemed to take forever to walk to that little church. When we finally reached it and they went in, the dog and I sat down out front.

It was nearly night now, and the candles inside the church were starting to glow through the open door. Over my head the stars came out, brighter than the candles. The night got darker and darker. Everything was so beautiful it hurt.

I felt bad in a whole new way. Somehow, telling Tehane and seeing her tears had made me feel lonelier than ever. I wouldn't have thought that would be so, if I'd thought about it at all.

"Dog," I said, "I am all alone on this earth. My family's dead and gone, my best friend is dead. Hell, I don't even know your name. What is your name, dog?"

He pushed his nose into my hand and whined.

CHAPTER SIX

Kwok

I promised Tehane that I'd come back, and spent the night at Anani's place. I woke up Anapa twice with my dreaming.

The next day I helped Anani run water through the ditches he'd dug in his orchard, and he gave me two francs.

While I watched the water run around the roots of the trees, I thought about my plan to kill Gun. I still had more than six dollars of sea pay. When I was done working, I went over to the Chinese store to see what might be for sale. In Papeete you couldn't buy any thing that shot for six dollars. Maybe here things would be a little cheaper.

The store was a white wooden building that said KWOK on a sign on the roof. There was some Chinese writing beside it, which I guessed said the same thing. There were little advertisements in French and Chinese tacked up beside the door.

I went in and it was about the neatest general store I ever had seen. Not an inch of space wasted, but not crowded either. It had every-thing you could want: canned goods, tools, clothes, even a few books in French.

The place was empty except for a young, light-skinned Chinese guy behind the counter. Still, I said *"Bonjour, tout le monde,"* to show I knew how to be polite.

"Bonjour, monsieur," the Chinese fellow said. "You wish for something?"

"You sell guns here?" I asked.

He cocked his eye at me.

"What did you have in mind?"

"Whatever I can get for six dollars," I said.

He laughed. "Bullets," he said. "If you don't need too many." Then he said, "You're an American?"

"Oui," I said.

"Then let's talk English," the Chinese said. "I don't get much chance to do it out here."

"Well, I'll be darned," I said. "Where are you from, partner?"

"All over. At least the worst parts of it," the fellow said. "Ulysses Kwok's the name."

"Joe Sloan from Los Angeles," I said.

On second look I could tell Kwok wasn't all Chinese. There was something else in him, like there was in me.

"California, huh?" Kwok said. "I was born at the Presidio up in San Francisco. Two Californians meeting up in Mataiea." Kwok laughed. "Small world."

"Small world," I agreed. "So since it's so small, how about making me a deal on a shooting piece?"

"I couldn't sell you a gun for less than twenty-five dollars," he said. "Anything good will run you a lot more."

"That's steep," I said.

"Everything on this island but the breadfruit comes from some-place else," he said. "And it all costs to bring it in. But the truth is I haven't got anything now anyway. There's not much call for guns in Tahiti."

"What about that one?" I said.

Hanging up on the wall behind Kwok's head was a big black Springfield rifle like the army used. It was nearly as tall as I was, and I knew it would kick like a mule, but whatever it hit would stay hit. It was only a single-shot weapon, but its huge bullet was a real argu-ment settler.

"I couldn't sell you that," Kwok smiled. "Family heirloom."

"Well, suppose I wanted something and could pay for it," I said. "What could you do for me?"

"What would you want?" he asked.

I'd been thinking that over. A pistol would be cheapest, but also the trickiest to use. You have to keep in practice all the time to be good with a pistol. A Winchester rifle was best at close range, but it could give you trouble. If the tube that held the ammo got a dent in it, the bullets wouldn't feed into the chamber. That left either a long-range rifle or a shotgun. A good shotgun would take Gun down bet-ter than anything else, if I could get close enough to use it.

"I was thinking maybe a twelve-gauge," I said.

"New, I could get you one for about five hundred francs," Kwok said. "Used, maybe four hundred."

I shook my head. That was eighty to a hundred dollars.

"Well, maybe something will turn up," Kwok said. "You never

know in my business. A lot of folks bring me things in trade. But, say, as long as you're here, stick around for a while. I haven't had a chance to talk to another California boy since I left the States."

He went over to a metal chest and pulled out a couple of bottles.

"Ever have a cola drink?" he asked me.

"What's that?" I said.

"The latest thing from home," he said. "Some of them have wine in them; some of them have other things. Mostly sugar and water and fizz. I carry two or three different kinds. Want to try one?"

I wasn't thirsty, but I was curious, so I took the bottle Kwok held out. The cola wasn't bad, but it wasn't like anything I'd ever drunk before.

Come to that, Kwok wasn't like anyone I'd met before.

"If it isn't too personal," I asked, "how'd you fetch up in Tahiti?"

"Living up to my American name, I guess," Kwok said. "Ulysses. My father named me after President Grant."

I didn't get it.

Kwok put down his bottle.

"Well, besides Grant, there was a famous sailor named Ulysses a long time back. Went to a war and took ten years to get home from it. I went traveling when I was just a bit older than you. Hawaii. Idaho. Hawaii again. Now here. Anyplace a store might go. You?"

"Grew up in Los Angeles on a little ranch," I said. "Lost the ranch to the railroad. My mama's dead, and my *abuelita*. My grandma. Daddy went off when we lost the ranch, so I went down to San Pedro and shipped out. That was two years ago. Seen a few things since then. Hawaii, Australia. Now here. But the Presidio, isn't that an army fort?"

"Was the last time I heard," Kwok said.

"So . . ."

"So how did I get born there? Easy. My father was in the army." Kwok grinned. "That's his old rifle. Sergeant Han Kwok. Pretty strange place to find a Chinese, maybe," Kwok said. "But he took to soldiering. Joined up in the Civil War and never got out. Always said our family was descended from a famous general back in the old days. Anyway, he married my mother in San Francisco. She was French."

"So that's how come you talk English like—" I began.

"Like an American?" Kwok laughed. "*Pourquoi pas, monsieur?*"

I laughed too.

"Will you be shipping out again?" Kwok asked.

"Not right away," I said. "Anani wants me to help him with his oranges."

"Anani. He's a good fellow," Kwok said. "Well, it's good talking with you. It's time for me to start closing up. Come back sometime. Sorry I can't help you about the gun."

"Suppose I got the money," I said. "Could you help me then?"

"Ask me again when you've got the money," Kwok said. "You can get anything in Tahiti if you've got the money. And I'm the guy who sells it."

"Thanks for the cola thing," I said.

I paused at the door. "By the way," I said. "Does a schooner called the *Mateata* ever drop anchor here?"

Kwok cocked his eye at me again.

"What do you have to do with the *Mateata*?" he asked.

"The captain owes me something," I said.

"Good luck getting it," Kwok said. "He owes me money too. Yeah, he stops here when he wants to. But not often. He usually goes into Papeete."

I whispered something under my breath.

"What?" said Kwok.

I hadn't realized I'd spoken aloud.

"Just something he said to me once," I said. "Sooner or later everyone pays what he owes."

"Well, the day he pays you I want to be standing in line with my hand out," Kwok said.

I went out.

So the White Wolf came here, but not often. It looked as if I had time to find the gun I needed. And Kwok might be a help to me or might not.

It was getting on toward night now. I headed back to Anani's house. But as I passed the Catholic church, Tehane stepped toward me out of the shadows.

"I was hoping to find you," she said in French. "Will you talk with me again?"

"Sure," I said.

"Let us go down to the beach," Tehane said.

The night was blue when we started, black when we got there, even though it was only a little way. Day and night come and go fast in the tropics.

"I loved Robert," she told me as we walked. "He was the only man I have ever loved."

And that was all she said for a while. Then she started talking about the way she'd met him and what he'd been like. How brave he'd been, and how smart. She poured out her stories, and I drank them up.

She'd been going to the French nuns' school when Robert came. They'd fallen in love and promised themselves to each other, but Tehane didn't want to get married until she'd finished her schooling. So he'd sworn to come back in two years and give up the sea.

"I wanted to be worthy of him," she said. "He knew so much. All I had was a talent for mathematics and a love for words. I didn't want to be an ordinary girl, married at thirteen, knowing only how to cook and raise babies. That would never be enough for Robert. I have been helping at the school for the last year, teaching calculus. I wanted him to see me teach. It would have made him proud."

Yes it would have, I thought. Any man would be proud of you.

"Did Robert tell you how we fell in love?" she asked me.

"No," I said. "All he ever told me was how much he loved you."

"He was like the answer to my prayers," she said. "My father was a ship's captain who retired here. Much older than my mother. He raised me to know there is much world beyond that reef. And he made me want to see it. Then Robert came, and I knew I wished to see it with him, wherever he went. And Robert told me . . . Robert told me that wherever I was his world was. And every word he spoke to me was true."

She was all talked out. We just stood side by side, watching the waves come and go on the beach.

"Now that you have done what you came to do, where will you go?" she asked at last.

"Well, *mademoiselle*, like I told you; I plan to kill Gun and the White Wolf if I can," I said.

I don't know what I'd expected, exactly. I know I thought she'd try to thank me somehow, maybe tell me how brave I was. What she said instead hit me like a cold wave.

"Do not waste your life. Nothing you can do will help Robert. Go on from here and make a new day for yourself."

"I can't do that," I said. "And I wouldn't if I could."

"Then you are a great fool," she said.

"Well, maybe I am," I replied. "But I know if it had been the other way around, Robert wouldn't let them gun me down and do nothing."

"If you let those men determine your life, you will become what they are," Tehane said. "If you want to honor Robert, leave Tahiti and never come back to it. Leave all this behind forever."

"And what about you?" I asked.

"I will mourn him," she said.

"That's all?" I said. "You think that's enough for Robert?"

"I think it is all there is," Tehane said.

"Well, it's not," I said. "And I'm staying right here until I get my chance to even the score."

"Leave," she said. "Leave Tahiti as soon as you can. For Robert."

From up in the town I heard a *himene* getting started. The song wasn't one I knew, but I could understand the words all right. It was a song about a warrior back in the old days who'd fought till his enemies killed him.

I started toward the sound. Tehane caught my arm. "That song is not for you," she said urgently. I shook her off.

"I'll be staying with Anani," I said.

Tehane stood there alone, watching me go.

"That song is not for you," she called after me.

CHAPTER SEVEN

A Savage Comes to Mataiea

Time went by slow and even, with every day like every other. I worked for Anani when he wanted me. He let me use his axes whenever I wanted, and I chopped wood for people to earn a little more. And I made a few francs working for Kwok when he needed help stocking shelves or sweeping or whatever. That got me looked down on by the other white folks. Any white man who'd work for a Chinese was as low-down as they came, so they thought. But what did I care? It's all the same in the grave. And slowly my little bit of money piled up toward that hundred dollars Kwok said I had to have.

One day Kwok asked if I wanted an extra job. "Just something I need done every once in a while."

"Sure," I said. "If it pays."

"It's an extra ten francs," Kwok said.

"What?" I asked.

He held out a strip of red cloth.

"Tie this to a coconut tree down by the beach just outside of town. One of the ones that's between the beach and that big *marae*."

I knew the place he meant.

"Any one of them?"

"Use the tallest," Kwok said.

"That's it? Tie this cloth around the tallest cocoa palm by the big *marae* outside town?"

"That's it. And don't ask any questions," Kwok added.

"How legal is it?"

"Since when is it illegal to tie a cloth around a tree?" Kwok said. "But just do it at night."

So that night I went out and climbed the tree and tied the cloth around it. I didn't feel scared so much as silly.

Kwok gave me my ten francs the next day, and it went into my gun fund.

After that, every few weeks as long as I stayed in Mataiea, I ran that errand for Kwok. Every time I went back to the coconut tree the red rag would be gone. I never asked why about any of it.

I didn't stay long at Anani's place. Anani and his family were good to me, but I was pretty bad company for them. Some nights I'd wake up the boys in the room with me, moaning or even screaming at another nightmare. And when I was awake, I wasn't exactly cheerful.

After a couple of weeks, when we were working in the oranges, Anani had a little talk with me.

"Totefa," he said. "You are a very good worker. I like having you here."

"Thank you," I said. "It's good to have something to do."

"I know you are sad, Totefa. Everyone in Mataiea knows why you are so full of tears and what you mean to do. Everyone except Minot the *gendarme*. I don't think anyone would tell him."

Minot was the one cop in Mataiea, and he acted as if he thought he was the whole Paris police force.

"But you are not easy to be with when you are not working, Totefa. Perhaps you need a place to be alone at night. No Tahitian would want that, but you are an American. You are different. Would you like a house of your own?"

Anani's family had extra houses. A lot of Tahitians did. Big families would all live together on the same patch of ground and build houses as they wanted them. When they were done with one, they just left it.

Mine was an ordinary place: one room, with log walls and a thatch roof, two doors and four windows. The front door looked out toward the reef, and the back door looked across the fields to Mount Aori. It seemed small for a whole family, but it was plenty big enough for me. I slung my hammock and I was home.

And Anani turned out to be right. Swinging in the hammock and hearing the waves all night seemed to calm my dreams. I began sleeping until day came in through the cracks in my walls.

Kwok helped me out with a small iron stove and a coffee pot.

"Housewarming presents," he said, and wouldn't take a franc for them. Once I'd stuck a few pegs in the walls and made window curtains out of an old dress Tehura gave me, I felt as if I belonged there.

Some of the other folks in town began to come by. I knew that they wanted to be friendly, and I tried to be nice; but when it turned out I wasn't interested in finding a girl or joining a church, they sort of left me alone.

All of them but Anapa. He would come by every day or two to say hi and talk story. It was what he did with everybody in town. He seemed to feel it was his job. It was real easy to be friends with Anapa because he didn't expect me to talk. He did it all. It was like Titi back in Papeete.

"*Ia orana*, Totefa, guess what happened to me today?" he'd start. And then he'd be off on some long yarn about everyone and everything that had crossed his path since I'd seen him last. I can't say it was interesting, but I got to liking the sound of his voice.

One day he said, "Do you know what, Totefa? Father is renting the big old house that our family used to live in. He's renting it to a Frenchman. He's coming from Papeete. I wonder why he's doing that. What do you think?"

"I think it's Anani's business," I said.

"No, but the Frenchman. Why would he come here? What do you think?"

"There are already plenty of Frenchmen in Mataiea," I said. "One more isn't going to make any difference."

"But this is a different kind of Frenchman," Anapa said.

"How is he different?"

"I don't know. He makes things," Anapa said. "Pictures. He's an *artiste*. What's an *artiste*, Totefa?"

Artiste, Anapa had said, because there's no word for *artist* in Tahitian. It sure sounded like my old friend Monsieur Paul Gauguin.

That was a surprise. I couldn't see why he'd want to come out to Mataiea, if it was him.

But Anapa was off on something else now.

"You know what, Totefa? A lady says you should come for dinner sometime. She says you spend too much time alone down here at your house."

"Wait a minute. Who's this lady, and why does she want to feed me dinner?" I asked.

"Tehane is the lady," Anapa said. "When do you want to come, Totefa? Tonight?"

Remembering how we'd parted last time I'd seen her and how we'd avoided each other since, I sure couldn't see why Tehane would be asking me to eat with her. And I was pretty sure I didn't want to.

"Maybe some time," I said. "Not tonight."

"But why? You're not doing anything tonight," Anapa said. "You never do anything."

"I know. Keeps me busy, doing so much nothing," I said. "I've got a full load of nothing on for tonight. That's why I can't come. Maybe someday when I don't have so much nothing, I'll make it up to the lady's place."

Anapa laughed hard. "Too much nothing! Too much nothing! I'll be busy too. From now on, I'll do too much nothing."

"Anyway, thank the *mademoiselle* for me," I said.

And Anapa went on to something else.

A couple of days later, a big wagon came slowly down the road. It was the kind we used to haul oranges to the ships in harvest time.

Right ahead of it was a little two-man buggy driven by Lieutenant Jénot. Gauguin was sitting beside him.

They bounced up to the old Anani house and stopped. Anani came out and met them, and they all waited for the big wagon to lumber up to join them.

I was watching all this from the back door of my place. There was no work to do in the grove that day, and Kwok didn't need me for anything. But as soon as the wagon stopped, Anani raised his arm and called me over.

"Totefa, come and help me. There is work to be done."

I went over slowly. I wasn't sure how I felt about helping *Monsieur le Artiste* move in. We'd parted company on decent terms, I guess. In fact, I was wearing the hat he'd given me. But I still thought he was pretty much a dude, and I didn't have much use for dudes.

Gauguin gave me a nod and a thin smile when I came up to him. He was wearing another hat, a big, black, floppy beret. A dude hat, I thought.

"*Ia orana*," he said, and went on in Tahitian, "it are good to see you. This is good place. Here I live and work and be happy."

That's how he talked Tahitian then, and he never got a whole lot better.

"*Ia orana*," I said. "Welcome to Mataiea."

Anani got two of his boys to help us, and we all pitched in unloading Gauguin's stuff. Even with six of us doing it, it took time. That man had brought half a dozen trunks, boxes and boxes of paint and varnish, cans of turpentine and fuel oil, a case of wood-carving tools, a guitar, a kind of horn I'd never seen and three other musical instruments besides, fishing rods, chairs, pots and pans, three different swords, and five different kinds of canvas—everything from rough stuff that could have been used to patch a sail to some that was almost as smooth as a cotton shirt. There were other canvases stretched on thin wooden frames. I wondered if he'd left anything behind for the people in France.

There was something else in all that cargo that caught my eye: a beautiful wooden case that had to hold either a rifle or a shotgun. Shotgun, I guessed by the length, though it could have been a Winchester, or maybe some kind of short rifle that they might have in France. I hoped I could find out more about that somehow.

When we had finally filled the place with everything from the wagon, Gauguin pulled a couple of bottles of wine out of a box and found some cups and offered us a drink all around.

"*Ia orana*," Gauguin said, raising his cup. "*Ia orana*, Tahiti. I be now in true heart this place. Papeete was bad. Papeete is no mana. All mana gone now from Papeete. Here I work. I live and be happy."

Mana is a kind of spirit stuff Tahitians believe in. It's not the same as soul and it's not the same as magic, but it's a little like both. Everything has it; and if you have a lot, you can send it out of yourself and into other things.

When we'd finished, Lieutenant Jénot stood up and handed Gauguin his cup.

"My friend, I would like to stay and help you to unpack, but duty calls. I must be back in Papeete tonight."

"I'll stay and help if you want," I said. I was hoping for a closer look at that gun.

But Jénot said, "Spare me a few moments," and beckoned me outside.

Away from the house, he said, "The Tahitians are still talking about Gun, the White Wolf, and Tehane Man. I wonder: Are you willing to help me, if the chance comes, to do something about those two?"

"If you can get me a gun," I said. "I'll kill them next time they come to Mataiea."

"That was not precisely what I had in mind," Jénot said. "Though your spirit is admirable. Warrior mana, as my friend would say. But to go on, one of my jobs here in Tahiti is military intelligence. You know what that is?"

I shook my head no.

"In a small way, I am a spy, and a master of spies," Jénot said with a little bow. "Through my spies I hear that, while this White Wolf spends most of his time cheating natives out of their copra crops, he may be involved in smuggling rifles from time to time. Often these are rifles that belong to France. If I could catch him at it, he, or both he and Gun, might end up in the prison of Devil's Island. Very bad place, Devil's Island. We call it the Dry Guillotine. Would that suit you?"

"Not even half," I said.

"Very well. In any case, would you send me word when he comes to Mataiea?" Jénot said. "It may mean nothing when he does so, or it may mean much. In any case, I try to keep track of him when he's in Tahiti."

"I will if I can," I said.

"Then let us be friends," Jénot said, and stuck out his hand.

I shook it, and he climbed into his gig and drove off.

I went back inside and started to help with the big things in Gauguin's pile of luggage. When those were done, Anani and his boys left. I stuck around, still hoping for a look inside that gun case.

"They call you Totefa," Gauguin said in French.

"Here in Mataiea they do," I said.

"You are American," Gauguin said.

"Sure am," I said. "From California. Los Angeles."

"American. Even so, there is something about you," Gauguin said. "Like mana. What do you think of your cup?"

I'd never seen anything like the cup he'd given me. It was made of clay and shone dark, shiny red. There was a strange face molded into it. It wasn't a human face. It had eyes like an angry cat and a grim mouth. It didn't look evil exactly, but it made me wonder what kind of thing it was supposed to be. It reminded me a little of the way I'd imagined Smoking Mirror.

"I made this," he said. "It is the head of a god. Not a god of Tahiti. A god of Peru. A jaguar god. When I was a small boy, I saw jaguars there."

"They have them in Mexico too," I said.

"What do you know of Mexico?" he said.

"I'm half Mexican," I said. "My *abuelita* taught me a lot of things about the old country."

"Do you speak Spanish?" he asked me.

"*Sí*," I answered. "*Mi abuelita me enseño eso tambien.*"

Gauguin looked at me as if I'd just grown wings.

"Spanish is the language I prefer above all others," he said. "You must come and speak with me. Often, I hope."

"I'm just down on the beach," I said. "I suppose we'll see something of each other."

He looked at me hard. Then he said, "I was right to come to Mataiea."

CHAPTER EIGHT

Little Friends

By the time we got Gauguin's stuff unpacked, he was Paul to me. You probably know how it is when you work together with someone you don't know very well. You start feeling friendlier than you would any other way. We worked the rest of the afternoon and into the evening. Gauguin lit a couple of lamps so we could keep going after sunset. He poured a lot more wine too. Most of it went into him.

All that time we talked Spanish. It was good to hear it again, even though Paul's was a different kind of Spanish than I'd heard before. Real flowery and full of big words. I guessed his people had to be pretty important down there in Peru.

He said he'd gone there when he was a baby to live with his mother and her family and come back to France when he was five.

"I have never forgotten those colors," he said. "Alive in themselves. Not like the sweet, pallid shades of Europe. Even the fog when it comes is something beautiful there. Do you know what they call the fog in Lima, Totefa? The pearly mist. Perhaps that is what drove me to be an artist. All my life I have been trying to find such colors again."

I told him about Los Angeles and the ranch and Abuelita and Mama. None of it sounded like much to me, but Paul hung on my words as if they were clues to a missing gold mine. I told him about shipping out and stopping in Hawaii for a while. I even told him about Robert and coming to Mataiea to find Tehane. The only thing I left out was that I wanted to borrow his shotgun to kill a couple of guys someday. I figured that could wait.

The funny thing was, the more I said, the more excited Paul got.

"We are so much alike, Totefa," he said. "You are one-half Mexican. I am one-quarter Peruvian. We both speak Spanish but live in countries that do not. We have both been sailors, and I was almost exactly your age when I first shipped out. But I will tell you the greatest thing we have in common: We are both savages."

"I'm no savage," I said. "I'm an American."

"That is because you are savage enough not to recognize it," he said. "You are from the Wild West, like Buffalo Bill. Civilization has touched you but not crushed you. I have spent most of my life in France, the most civilized place on earth."

He poured another glass of wine into his red goblet and went on.

"You know, Totefa, after I left the navy, I went into the stock exchange. I made a great deal of money, and my wife enjoyed spending every franc of it. We lived well. But not for one day did I have the feeling that what I was doing mattered. Inside me was always the memory of the sun of Peru and the shadows of its palms. The blood of the Incas flows in my veins, and the blood of the Aztecs does in yours. And I feel it more strongly, having been made more civilized. Our blood rebels against the frauds of everyday life."

Then he said, "Were you ever in a war?"

"That's a funny question," I said. "No."

"I was," he said. "My last berth was on the *Jérome Napoleon*. She was the personal yacht of Napoléon III, but she was a hell-ship for the crew. When the war with Prussia started in 1870, the navy put guns on her and sent her to blockade their coast. Since they would not come out to fight, it did not matter that our guns were placed wrong. The one time we fired at an enemy he got away because our cannons couldn't be aimed at him. And that was my war."

"Did you whip the Prussians?" I asked.

He snorted.

"We of the navy did our part, but it was really a land war. The Prussians crushed our army, and nothing we did mattered. We sailed home, and the crew was given indefinite shore leave. I never came back from mine. I suppose I am still on a crew roster somewhere. So, Totefa, in a way I am a deserter. A deserter whom no one really wants.

"We have declined, Totefa," he went on. "The warrior has become the soldier. The hunter has become the businessman. The chief has become the provincial administrator. From all this I have deserted. I asked myself, Where do we come from? What are we? Where are we going? And I deserted. For I know there remains one road by which a man may reclaim his savage purity. That is art. I will prove this. I will prove it here, in Mataiea."

"I don't understand very well," I said.

"I would estimate that you are one-quarter civilized while I am one-quarter savage," he said to me. "That is why you do not feel the truth of what I say. But it does not matter. To find you here in Mataiea is a miracle. You will have much to teach me, I think. And it may be that I will have something to teach you. Your health, Totefa."

I reckoned he must have been drunker than he looked to go on talking like that, but I loved the sound of it. Listening to Paul was like stepping out of life and into a story. Or maybe like stepping into real life for the first time.

We were done with the unpacking. The house was so crowded I didn't see where Paul was going to sleep. His big easel stood in one corner like the lord of the house, with all the boxes of paints and bolts of canvas clustered at its feet like servants or children.

"It is time to bring out my little friends," he said.

He opened an old tin box with a picture of a girl eating cookies on it. Inside were postcards, which he started pinning up on the walls beside the easel. There were all kinds. Pictures of paintings and statues, photographs, people's visiting cards.

"What are these?" I asked. "Paintings of yours, any of them?"

"These are my little friends," he said. "Sometimes they talk to me. Sometimes they help me with my paintings. But no, none of them are mine. I have not yet achieved the dignity of being transformed into a postcard."

There was one photograph of a girl and four boys. The girl was real pretty.

"Who is she?" I asked.

"My daughter, Aline," Paul said.

"Pretty," I said. "The name, I mean. The name and the girl."

"She is beautiful, and she has always been beautiful," Paul said. "If you were to meet her in a few years when she is as old as you are now, she would break your heart."

"Is she back in France?" I asked.

"No," he said, and I could tell he was hurt. "She and her brothers are with their mother. In Denmark."

He almost spat the last word.

"A cold, damp, abysmal place, full of cold, damp, abysmal people. But when my paintings sell, I will bring them all back to me. Even my wife."

"Oh. That'll be good." I didn't know what more I could say. I could tell the separation was hurting him like a hot knife.

To change the subject, I said, "Is that your wife?"

One of the little friends was a picture of a beautiful woman lying on a bed, wearing her hair up and nothing else but a ribbon around her neck and a slipper.

Paul laughed.

"Wife? Ah, Totefa, you are truly the voice of the ancient, noble world. No, her name is Olympia. Or rather, the painting is so named. Her name is Victorine Meurent. Eduoard Manet painted her, and she became famous for being Olympia. Now no one recalls her, and Olympia is still famous. That is the power of art, Totefa."

He pointed to one of the other pictures. It was of a statue of part of a man.

"What do you think he was doing when he was whole?" Paul asked.

"I'd say he was chopping wood," I said. "The way the shoulders go up, I think he had an ax over his head."

"Excellent. You see? This statue from a Greek temple is universal, even in fragments. Even to you, who have never seen a Greek temple. The savage in you recognizes its truth."

"I chop a lot of wood," I said.

He squeezed my shoulder and smiled at me.

"*Salvaje*," he said. "Savage."

Paul got up and went out into the night. I followed him. He raised his cup to the night sky, to the stars and the moon and the shining clouds. There was no sound but the silvery rustle of the cocoa palms and the faint thud of the surf.

"I am home," he said.

There were tears on his face.

"Paul, *amigo*, where are your own paintings?" I asked.

He waved an arm back toward the easel standing proud in the lamplight.

"They are there," he said. "Waiting to be born."

Then he hugged me. I was surprised, but I hugged him back.

"I will paint such things as have not been seen in Europe, Totefa," he said. "I will capture all these colors and make them breathe on canvas. I will paint the world new, as it was at the creation, when everyone saw with savage eyes. You will see. You and I will be the first to see."

All of a sudden he went kind of limp. He let go of me, bent over, and grabbed his stomach.

"Paul, are you all right?" I asked.

"Yes. I will be," he answered. "Help me in, *amigo.*"

I slung his arm around my neck and helped him up the two steps to his door.

"I have a hammock," he said, and pointed to it.

I hung it in the corner opposite the easel, and he rolled into it.

"Good night, Totefa," he mumbled. "Thank you."

"Good night, Paul," I said, and put out the lamps and left.

Walking back to my place, I still felt as though I'd stepped into a story or a song. Maybe one of the deep, pounding story tunes the Tahitians sang about the old times.

And it wasn't until I got back to my place that I realized I'd forgotten all about his gun, or even needing a gun, for the first time since Robert had been killed.

CHAPTER NINE

The Pink Coral Jail

I was still asleep when Anapa came by.

"Wake up, Totefa, wake up! I have a story for you. It just happened."

"What?" I said, rubbing my face. "Did a coconut fall?"

"No, no," he said, laughing. "A real story. You know that new Frenchman? He's in jail."

"Huh?" I said, wide awake now.

"Tehane went down to the stream to wash some clothes, and what did she see? The Frenchman was in there, washing himself. Where everyone could see it. And, Totefa, he wasn't wearing any clothes."

"What did Tehane do?" I asked.

"She ran away and got the *gendarme*," Anapa said.

That sounded bad. Gendarme Minot was not only mean, but bored. In a place such as Mataiea, there just wasn't much for him to do. I didn't doubt he'd haul Paul off to jail for less than skinny-dipping.

"I'd better go see about it," I said, pulling on my clothes.

"Is the *artiste* a friend of yours?" Anapa asked.

"Yes. I think so. Yes," I said.

"What will you do?" Anapa asked.

"I don't know yet. Minot's kind of a hardhead," I said.

When we got down to the jail, I could hear voices shouting in French.

"Dog!"

"Insupportable!"

"Authority!"

"Fool! Beast!"

I knocked on the door of the little coral building. Then, when no one answered, I just went in. Anapa followed me.

Paul was hanging on the bars of his cell. He had on his clothes, including his beret. Minot was across the room, waving a law book at him.

"Totefa," Paul shouted when he saw me. "Trust the French to put a policeman in the garden of Eden."

"Get out! Get out!" Minot shouted, waving his law book at Anapa and me.

"Paul, I heard you were . . . swimming without your clothes," I said. "They don't do that here. Not where anybody can see them. Tell him you didn't know."

"He knows I didn't know," Paul said. "It doesn't matter to him. His precious authority is all he cares about. If I don't pay fifty francs, I stay here for a week. Go and get my sketchbook and pencils."

"Why don't you just pay him the money?" I asked.

"Fifty francs is too much," Paul said. "Five francs would be too much. I have done nothing wrong. Besides, *amigo,* I don't have fifty francs at the moment," he added in Spanish.

Now Minot was putting down his law book and picking up his stick. He pointed it at me.

"Get out."

I could tell he wanted to use it, so I backed out, pushing Anapa along.

Outside, I thought hard. I had about a hundred francs. I could give half of it to get Paul out. But that was a big chunk of gun money, and I didn't want to break into my gun money even for Paul. It would be like betraying Robert.

Maybe Paul's friend Lieutenant Jénot would help, if I could get a letter to him. But that was at least a two-day wait.

"My sketchbook, Totefa. I'll go mad here without it," Paul bellowed.

I started walking back toward Paul's house, feeling rotten. If I gave him the money, I was letting down my dead friend; if I didn't I was backstabbing my living one. And I was worried that Paul and Minot might get into it bad if they had a whole week together. And a pencil against a billy club didn't seem like much of a fight.

"It's too bad Tehane had to see that," Anapa said. "If she hadn't, none of this would have happened."

I stopped.

"Anapa, that was a very smart thing you just said," I said.

"I know," he said. "I say smart things all the time. Why is it smart?"

"Where's Tehane?" I said.

"At home," Anapa said.

"Let's go over there," I said.

Tehane was hanging out clothes when we got there. She waved and went on working while Maria called to me, "Did you hear what happened to Tehane this morning, Totefa?" and went over the whole story again.

I listened as if I hadn't heard it already from Anapa, to be polite. Maria put in some touches that Anapa had left out. Paul had frightened Tehane. When she saw him, he'd just turned and looked back at her. He hadn't smiled, or tried to hide. I remembered that stare of his. It could frighten a person.

But still, he didnt belong in jail for it.

"*Ia orana*, Tehane," I said, going over to the clothesline.

"*Ia orana*," she said. "It has been a long time."

"I'm sorry I never came to dinner," I said.

She nodded.

"We didn't part well," I said.

"No."

We didn't seem to be going anywhere with this conversation, so I changed it.

"I hear you . . . saw the new Frenchman."

She nodded again.

"He's in jail now," I said.

"Good," Tehane said.

"I'm afraid for him," I said. "He's got a hot temper. So has Minot. He's in for a week. I'm afraid of what Minot may do to him if they get too angry in there."

"Why do you care?" she asked.

"I kind of like him," I said. "He doesn't seem like a bad man. Just foolish, maybe. He wants Tahiti to be some place it's not."

"Well now he will learn what kind of place it is," she said.

"Tehane, would you be willing to help him get out?" I asked.

"What? Why? No," she said all at once.

"Tehane, he thinks Tahiti is like the Garden of Eden," I said. "He was just doing what he imagined people did out here away from Papeete."

"No!"

"I'll bet if you told Minot that you thought you were mistaken, he'd have to let Paul go," I said.

"But I am not mistaken!"

"I know you're not. But if you say you are, he can go free. And he'll still know better. Isn't that the point?" I said.

"No. I did not like the way he looked at me," Tehane said.

"I didn't like the first look he gave me either," I said. "Or the second. Or the one after that. Don't judge him by looks, Tehane. Listen to him talk first. Please."

"No," she said. "I won't lie."

"Tehane, how will you feel if something bad happens to Paul while he's in Minot's jail?" I said.

She didn't answer. She went on hanging up clothes, and the only time she opened her mouth was to take a clothespin out of it.

I just sat there. I didn't think saying anything more would help. Anyway, I didn't have anything more I could say.

When she was done, she said to me, "All right. Let's go. I am ready to lie for you."

So back we went to jail, Tehane and me, and Anapa. And when we got there, Tehane said she had been mistaken about what she'd seen.

I sure did admire the way she did it. Stood with her back straight and looked Minot right in the eye and unsaid everything she'd said before. Even I almost believed her.

"You are quite certain, *mademoiselle*?" Minot asked, sounding very unhappy. "Because you were quite certain before."

"Yes. I am certain," she said. "I had never seen so much of a white man before. And no one bathes there anyway. It surprised me. But I realize now that I was wrong."

Minot's face got red over the collar of his uniform. He didn't say anything for a long time. Then at last he got up, took his keys, and went back to the cell.

A minute later, he came back with Paul. Paul gave the three of us the same look I'd seen on his face at Pomare's funeral: the tilted head and the gaze from under his heavy eyelids. Then he nodded.

"*Ia orana, amigo,*" he said. "It is good to see you again. Very good. Though I see you did not bring me my sketchbook. No matter."

Then he bowed to Tehane. "*Mademoiselle,* I am deeply in debt to your graciousness."

Tehane nodded and raised her chin.

"Come, my friends," Paul said. "A savage set free must celebrate. Let us go to the store of the Chinese. Please feel free to bankrupt me."

We headed over to Kwok's. And as we came up to it, the door opened and the two men on earth I hated came out. The White Wolf was wearing a light-colored suit, and his beard was cut. Gun looked just like Gun.

I felt a rage in me that made me stand stone still. I couldn't move. Here they were, and I couldn't move.

The White Wolf held out his hand to Paul.

"*Bonjour,* Monsieur Gauguin," he said. "I am pleased to meet you again."

"*Bonjour,* Captain Arnaud," Paul said. "How do you come to be in Mataiea?"

"A brief visit on business," the White Wolf said. "Indeed, I am leaving now for another cruise to the outer islands. One day you must accompany me there."

"One day I shall, gladly," Paul said. "*Au revoir.*"

"*Au revoir,*" the White Wolf said.

All this time, Gun kept his eyes on Paul. I could see he didn't recollect me any more than the White Wolf did. Oh, I thought, why hadn't God given me a gun this day? I'd never have as good a chance to get them both.

They moved off, down to the beach, and it was only when they were beyond rifle range that I knew Tehane was standing beside me with her hand on my arm.

"That's the White Wolf," Anapa said. "He's a bad man. Do you like him, Monsieur Gauguin? Is he a friend of yours."

"I met him in Papeete," Gauguin said. "No, he is not a friend. But I like to listen to his tales of the copra trade. I am sure he exaggerates his adventures, and I know a rogue when I smell one. But old sailors are often rogues, and I like to speak of the sea."

He went into the store. I started to follow him, but Tehane pulled me back.

"Tell him nothing; show him nothing," she whispered.

I nodded, and we followed Paul.

Kwok looked furious, but he put on a smile when he saw us.

"*Bonjour*, Mademoiselle Tehane; *bonjour*, Anapa, *bonjour*, Joe. *Bonjour* Monsieur. Welcome to Kwok's."

Paul nodded stiffly to Kwok's greeting. Then he stood to one side while Anapa went straight to the candy case, and Tehane, after she'd taken a look at cloth and small pretties, went over to the shelf of books.

I had to hand it to her. She was as cool as spring water, acting as if nothing had happened. I tried to do the same.

Kwok went behind the counter and took down the big old rifle. He started polishing the stock.

"Did you get your money from The White Wolf?" I asked.

"Who's your friend?" he asked me in English, ignoring my question.

"Paul Gauguin. He's an *artiste*. Just got here," I said.

"*Artiste*, huh?" Kwok said. "We've been needing one of those here in Mataiea."

"What's wrong with being an *artiste*?" I said.

"Nothing," Kwok said. "And there's nothing wrong with being an *artiste* who hates Chinese. I just don't like it much, that's all."

"He hasn't said anything, has he?" I said.

"No, he hasn't," Kwok said. "He hasn't said anything. Not even '*bonjour*.' I've been Chinese all my life. I know when white folks don't like us yellow folks." Then he smiled. "Doesn't matter," he said. "Guys like that don't make life any harder. He better not ask me for credit, that's all."

"He's just that way," I said. "I didn't like him at first either. He gets better. Trust me."

"Oh, I trust you," Kwok said. "But I wouldn't trust him too far if I were you."

I couldn't figure out what that meant. Maybe it had something to do with the White Wolf. Anyway, I could tell Paul wanted to talk to me, so I excused myself and went over to him.

"Totefa, these prices are obscene," he whispered in Spanish. "Worse than Papeete. This man is the biggest pirate ashore."

"There's no more honest man in Tahiti," I said. "Everything's expensive here because it comes from somewhere else."

"So I discovered in Papeete," Gauguin said. "That was one reason why I came here. But how am I to afford gifts for the two of them? I can barely afford candy for the boy. What are their names, by the way?"

"The boy's Anapa," I said. "Tehane's his cousin."

"How old?" Paul asked.

"He's eleven, she's fifteen, sixteen," I said. "Why?"

"Fifteen," he said. "At that age they want the world."

Anapa might not have wanted the world, but he sure meant to clean Kwok out of candy. He was stacking up fistfuls of it on the counter.

Paul looked at what was going on and went over to Tehane.

"You are finding something to your taste, *mademoiselle*?" he asked.

Tehane was holding the biggest book on the shelf. It said *Les Miserablés* on the cover.

"I have heard this is excellent," she said. "Sister Elizabeth says Victor Hugo is the finest writer in the French language, even if he is a heretic. But I fear it is very expensive."

"He is certainly the longest writer in the French language," Paul said. "I wonder what else is here? Ah."

He took down a little book not one quarter the size of the one Tehane held.

"*Le Bateau Ivre*," he said. "Rimbaud. Now this is great. And it is modern. Imagine finding such a book here."

"*The Drunken Boat*? But why should a boat be drunken?" Tehane asked.

"Drunk with beauty, perhaps. Or with mystery," Paul said. "This man writes as I mean to paint. And if I painted as Hugo wrote, I should need canvas the size of a mainsail, on which I would draw political cartoons."

"But why should a boat be drunk with anything?" Tehane asked.

"Perhaps that is what you are meant to find out," Paul said. "Excuse me a moment."

Paul went over and talked to Kwok.

I decided Kwok had been right—Paul didn't like him at all. He held himself as far away as he could and still talk quietly. And I was pretty sure I knew what he was talking about. He wanted to know if Kwok would let him owe the money for whatever book Tehane picked out. And I already knew the answer to that.

I sneaked a look at the price written inside the cover of *Le Bateau Ivre*. High.

"Let me count the pages on that other one, Tehane," I said. "I've never seen a book that big before, not even a Bible."

She handed it over and I got a look at the price, and winced.

Looking back over at Paul, I saw Kwok raise his hands and shake his head.

Well, this was going real bad. Anapa was getting his mountain of candy, but it was Tehane who deserved to be thanked. And it wasn't going to happen unless I did something about it.

I went over to Kwok.

"I can cover for Paul," I said. "Bring you the money this afternoon."

Kwok nodded. "Which book?"

I gulped. "Both of them."

It was more than the fifty francs I would have had to pay to spring Paul from jail. But what else could I do?

Then I had another idea.

"You don't have to pay me back, Paul. Just let me use your shotgun once in a while," I said.

"Agreed," Paul said. "Agreed between warriors."

So Anapa got his candy, Tehane got her books, and I had my way to kill when the next chance came. Money well spent, I guessed.

We all walked out of the store together. Tehane held her books as if they were a treasure or maybe a baby, and Anapa chonked down his candy happy as a pig in clover.

Paul walked along silently a little behind Tehane. His fists were clenched. He seemed angry, but why? He was out of jail, wasn't he?

We came to the place where she turned off for home.

"Thank you," she said quietly. "I have never been given two books at once before."

Paul smiled.

"You are most welcome, *mademoiselle*," he said. "Surely, the authors have never been held in more beautiful arms. I hope you enjoy the Rimbaud especially."

"I hope I will enjoy them both," Tehane said, and started up the path to her place. Anapa skipped along beside her.

"I've eaten all the candy in Tahiti!" he shouted.

"Thank you, Totefa, for making it possible for me to thank the *mademoiselle*," Paul said.

"Sure thing," I said. "Thanks for the loan of the shotgun."

"I realize now that I do not even know her surname," Paul said.

"De Pouning," I said.

"You know her well?" Paul asked. "You are close?"

"Well, we're not close in the regular way," I said. "But I guess I know her as well as I know anybody in Mataiea."

"Well enough to persuade her to save me from Minot, at any rate," Paul said.

"Yeah," I said. "But we're not, you know, sweethearts or anything."

Paul nodded and smiled.

"A good day," he said. "A very good day, thanks to you, Totefa. Come by my house tonight if you like, and we will drink wine. We will celebrate liberty, beauty, and friendship."

"Okay," I said.

Paul headed back to his place. I hurried down to my shack to get the money to pay Kwok.

But when Paul was a good way off, Anapa came scampering back to me.

"Tehane says to say she knows who really got her the books," he said.

CHAPTER TEN

Color and Canvas

I saw a lot of Paul after that. I'd go by whenever I was working for Anani and listen while he talked story about art, Peru, the ancient world, and how we were both savages. It was like being in a story he was making up as he went along, and I was part of it, a big part.

I told him more and more about my life, which had never seemed like anything much up to now. He'd take it, turn it in his hands like a piece of wood, and show me the shape of it. It made me feel for the first time as if it mattered that I was alive. The only thing I never told him about was Robert. Since he knew the White Wolf, that didn't seem smart, even if they weren't friends.

I even shared Smoking Mirror with him, which I'd never told anybody about but Abuelita. I was kind of afraid he'd laugh at me, but of course he didn't.

"Smoking Mirror?" he said when I finally told him. "That's a good name for the old devil. I know him well. He's the one who stole my job on the stock market and took my family from me. But I think your *abuelita* was right. Something is left behind. In my case, it is art.

Perhaps by destroying one life he has liberated me to a truer one."

He spent his days sitting on the front step of his house carving faces in wood. Sometimes they were human faces, sometimes they weren't. When he was done with one, he'd put it on a shelf near the little friends. In a couple of weeks, he had quite a collection. They looked as if they came to life at night and talked. I reckoned Abuelita would have crossed herself if she'd seen them.

But I wanted to see paintings, and one day I told him so.

"I will start as soon as I can," he said. "Unfortunately, the story of my encounter with Mademoiselle Tehane has spead all over Mataeia. People have decided that I am mad. When I ask them to pose, they smile and shake their heads. If Mademoiselle Tehane would agree, I'm sure others would. But she refuses me. Even that boy Anapa says no. But I am patient. It may be that I am not ready to paint all this. I am still ripening."

"Ripening?" I asked. "You mean like a coconut or something?"

"Exactly like that," Paul answered, flicking away a bit of wood from the stock he was holding. "Like a banana. Everything here ripens into great fullness. And so am I. I feel it. These colors around us are coming inside me. But the savage in me is not yet free. He can only look out through my eyes. He cannot yet work through my hands. Not in paint. But the knife. He understands the knife always. You see here, Totefa? With the knife he carves himself."

He put down the head he was working on and studied it. It looked like Anani, but fierce and grim. Maybe it was supposed to be Anani's grandfather. Maybe it was Anani the way Paul thought he should look, or the way Paul saw him.

"But, Paul, you painted back in Papeete, didn't you? I mean, Jénot told me you'd been sent out here to paint things for the government."

Paul barked a laugh.

"Government official? Yes, they gave me the title, but restrained themselves from giving me a salary. But I had hopes that my offical standing would get me work. And it did, a little. One fellow hired me to do a portrait of his wife. But I could think of nothing when I looked at her. She was ordinary. Flat as canvas. Finally I painted her with a sort of Japanese mask for a face, artificial as she was. Her husband took one look at it and refused to pay me."

He sighed and put down the head.

"How many greens do you see, Totefa?" he asked.

"Well, there's the cocoa palms, and the orange trees, and the breadfruits, and . . . I don't know. Six?"

"Six?" Paul said. "Totefa, every one of those things you spoke of has at least six greens all its own. The greens of dawn are not the greens of noon, and the greens of evening are different again. And if there is a shadow on one part and not on another, there are two greens on the same leaf. A man could study green here forever. And that is only one color. And before I can paint them, I must see them. I will paint no more masks."

"It's too bad you can't paint at night," I said. "Not so many colors then."

Paul gave me a look, then a laugh. "Totefa, my magnificent savage! You have shown me the way to begin. Is there not a meeting of Catholics tomorrow night?"

"There's going to be a *himene* over by the church," I said. "Same as usual."

"That shall be my subject," he said. "I will sit in the shadows and paint the singing."

He got up and went into the house.

"None of these are the size I want," he said, looking at the little stack of canvases ready to use. "Leave me for a while, Totefa, my genius. I must prepare a canvas."

"Can't I watch?" I said.

"There is nothing to see," Paul said.

"There is if you've never seen it," I said. The truth was, I didn't want to go and leave that feeling I always had when I was with him, that my life was bigger and realer than at any other time.

"Very well. Why not?"

Paul went into the house and got five pieces of wood. Then with a little saw he carefully trimmed a triangular piece off one long side of a piece and nailed it to the opposite side. The triangular piece ran along the uncut side like a little half roof. Then he did the same with one more piece. He nailed pieces into an oblong and put the fifth piece in the middle of the long sides for support. Then he measured the diagonals to make sure they were the same, and the corners of the frame were square.

"Hold this," he said.

I did, while he carefully lifted a piece of canvas out of a small pile. Then he laid the frame on it and tacked the canvas on one side with a little hammer.

"They say a real artist is a man who can stretch his own canvas," Paul said. "Now watch me make a jewel."

He went on tacking down the canvas until there was a diamond shape in the middle of it.

"Now, Totefa, we must be deft," he said. "This canvas must be stretched perfectly, so that it will hold its tension forever. And in this damp heat that will not be easy. A canvas that has been prepared for painting is almost a living thing. Sometimes I think I can hear it breathing."

Slowly Paul tacked the canvas down along the frame's long sides, putting in nails every couple of inches. When he was done, he tapped the canvas with his fingers. It sounded like a drum being stroked. He held it up in one hand, and for a second he looked like an ancient warrior with his shield.

"See, Totefa? A sail. I am still a sailor. But these sails can go where no mere ship ever could."

"So now you're ready?" I asked.

"Now I must paint it with gesso to make a base for the picture," he said. "By tomorrow it will be dry; and by tomorrow night, I will have the images I need to make it live."

CHAPTER ELEVEN

Himene

Paul and I waited for the *himene* to start before we went over to the church. Paul reckoned that he'd get better pictures if he waited until things were going strong.

And they sure were when we got there. Those singers almost made the ground shake.

Paul sat himself down just beyond the edge of the firelight. He crossed his legs and set up a big sketchpad in front of him. Sitting sideways to the *himene,* he had a little light on his paper.

"*Hasta la vista,*" I said. "I'm going over to the singing."

Paul didn't answer. He was already looking and drawing.

Tehane and Anapa saw me. They were sitting together in the middle of the group. Tehane raised her hand, and I went over and sat down.

"Why is he here?" she whispered.

"To draw," I said.

"It does not seem friendly," Tehane said.

"Maybe he's not friendly in the regular way," I said. "But if I were shipping out again, he's the guy I'd want to ship with."

We sang until the moon went down. By the time the *himene* was over, a lot of people had dropped out and were sleeping on the ground.

I felt good, the way I always felt after singing. As if I'd sung out everything that was wrong inside me, if only for a little while. I stood up and stretched and almost touched the stars.

"Walk with me back to my house," Tehane said.

We started back that way. Paul met us coming out of the dark.

"*Ia orana,* Mademoiselle Tehane," he said. "Have you read the Rimbaud?"

"I have read both the books," she said, looking at me. "I liked *Les Misérables* very much."

"But not the Rimbaud?" Paul said.

"It did not seem to me to be honest," she said. "*Les Misérables* is honest. I prefer things that are honest."

Paul stroked his chin. Then he said, "What you have said makes perfect sense. I had overlooked the fact that to a young woman such as you, a *belle sauvage,* Rimbaud's desire to recapture the primitive and true would be meaningless."

It was all over my head. All I knew was that I was impressed with Tehane for getting through *Les Misérables* in only a couple of weeks. That thing was more than thirteen hundred pages long.

"How did the drawing go?" I asked.

"In a few days I may have something to show you, Totefa," he said. "I will let you know when it is ready. Perhaps you, *mademoiselle,* would care to see it as well."

"Perhaps," she said. "Good night, Monsieur Gauguin."

We went on, and Paul went back into the dark.

Our path took us under a grove of palms the wind blew, and a coconut thunked down into the bushes.

"Do you know why Tahitian women keep a light burning all night when we sleep alone?" she asked me.

"No," I said.

"It is because of the *tupapus*," she said. "The evil dead. During the day, they stay up there on top of the mountain, plotting what they are going to do to us when night comes and they have power to come down among us again. I think Monsieur Gauguin is a kind of *tupapu*."

"You're wrong," I said. "He's just different. He's different from anybody I ever met. I'm beginning to think I like him as much as I liked Robert."

"He is nothing like Robert!" Tehane said.

"Well," I said. "This might make you think a little differently about him: When I'm around him, I forget all about Gun and the White Wolf."

"Robert can never come back to us," she said.

"Don't I know it?" I said. "Every day I think about that time I ran into the White Wolf and Gun outside Kwok's and didn't have so much as a wooden gun."

Tehane slapped me. I stood there, too surprised to be angry. I put my hand to my cheek.

Then she said, "Poor Totefa. You have been alone your whole life."

All of a sudden, Tehane was in my arms and I was kissing her and something lurched inside me and spread all through me, and it was my own life, and I didn't want to kill anybody, and I sure didn't want to die.

After a while, I said, "I'd better take you back to your house."

"No," she said, and kissed me again.

CHAPTER TWELVE

Painting Singing

I'd never had a girl of my own before. It was funny how it changed everything. I realized now that I'd wanted to die after Robert had been killed. That was why I'd been so anxious for a showdown with Gun. Now, I still wanted revenge, if I could get it, but I wanted to be around after I'd got it. Life was too sweet all of a sudden to throw it away. It was like every single thing was filled with love, and Tehane and I were in it and it was in us. We were always together, either at my place or at hers; and when I was there, Maria was almost as glad as Tehane was.

I forgot about everything else, even Paul. I didn't even wonder how the painting was coming. Then, after about a week that went by like no time at all, he came by my place one morning and asked me if I wanted to see it.

I was cutting some firewood. I meant to get enough for the next week for Anani's family and for me, to pay for the loan of the ax. Then I'd go cut some for Maria.

Tehane was inside, cleaning some fish. She hadn't moved in with me the way a lot of Tahitians moved in together when they became sweethearts, but she wanted to see I ate well.

I don't know if we were engaged exactly. But no one had ever been more important to me, not even Robert. In a way she'd saved my life, along with Paul. If I'd been a little older, if I'd had some money, I think I'd have asked her to marry me. But maybe it was too soon. Robert had only been dead a few weeks, and I knew she still loved him. I wanted her to love me at least as much as she loved Robert.

But now here was Paul with his hands smeared with paint and his fishing rods over his shoulder.

"I have finished the painting, Totefa," he said. "Come over and see it."

"Sure, I'll come," I said. "Can I bring Tehane?"

"*Mademoiselle* is always welcome," Paul said. "My felicitations on your new love. Love, and you will be happy."

Then he went on his way over to Kwok's. I knew why he was carrying his fishing tackle. He was going to trade it for canned goods or wine. Money was always tight for him.

Tehane didn't want to come at first.

"I do not care what he paints," she said. "It is not important to me."

"Come anyway," I said. "Maybe you'll like it. You never know."

Finally she said, "I will come, but only so that you do not spend all day with him, as I know you would if I let you."

I didn't much like the sound of that; but I was getting my way, so I didn't say any more.

We went by that afternoon, with Tehane's old dog in tow.

"Ah, the entire Tahitian Academy of Art, I see," Paul said when he saw us. "I had not expected my unveiling to attract so much interest."

The dog sat down and scratched.

"No matter," Paul said. "Every critic is a dog at heart."

The painting was up on the easel under a cloth.

"Here it is," he said. "My first true Tahitian painting."

He pulled aside the cloth.

I didn't know what I was looking at. It sure wasn't what I had expected to see. The palms looked about right, but everything else looked wrong. The painting was just bits of blue paint for the sky, white for the fire, and singers looking more like little dolls than like people.

"Well, my friend?" Paul said to me after a while.

"It's pretty," was all I could think of to say.

"Is it true?" Paul said.

I didn't say anything.

"Totefa, I want your truth," Paul said.

"Well, Paul," I finally said. "It doesn't look real."

"What do you mean?" he asked.

"I mean—it doesn't look like those," I said, waving at the little friends.

Paul didn't say anything for a while. Then he picked up a half-full bottle of wine and drained it.

"My poor Totefa," he said. "I know the kind of thing you expected to see. France produces that kind of art by the wagonload. Everything is perfect. Everything shines. And everyone knows that

that is art because there are very official gentlemen to tell them what art is. And they send this art around the world; and people in far places, where art is still true, believe what they see."

"Let me take another look at it," I said.

So I did. But no matter how hard I looked at it, it didn't look real.

Tehane was standing away from the painting, almost out of the room. It was about where Paul would have been when he was painting, figuring for scale. She had stared into the painting without saying a word ever since Paul had dropped the cloth. Now she said, "You have painted the singing. You have painted the songs."

Tehane started to go around, picking up Paul's cups and sculptures. She stared into them, turned them this way and the other, rubbed her fingers gently into their cracks, and put them down as if she were handling babies.

Paul watched her as if he was waiting for the most important word he would ever hear.

"You make beauty," she said finally. "You make things that are alive in their beauty."

"*Merci, mademoiselle,*" Paul said, and bowed. "You have seen. You have understood. The savage eye sees clearly."

Tehane curled her lip a little. She didn't like being called a savage. But Paul didn't seem to notice. He walked to the doorway and looked up at Aori.

"I will paint that mountain next," he said. "I think that will be easier to understand."

"What will there be to understand?" Anapa said. "It's just Aori."

"It is too bad you were born in Tahiti, young man," Paul said.

"You would have had a great future in the Paris art world. You and your dog."

Paul was angry that I hadn't liked the painting. But what could I do? He'd said he wanted my truth.

I decided it was time to leave.

"Let's go," I said. "Come on by tonight for dinner, Paul. We'll have fish."

"What do you say, *mademoiselle*? Will you be there?" Paul asked.

Tehane game me a hard look. But she said, "*Oui, monsieur.* I will come. But I hope I will not disappoint you by being insufficiently savage."

"*Mademoiselle,* you could never disappoint," Paul said.

"You are right, Totefa, we must go," Tehane said, and led the way out of Paul's house.

"Well, what do you think of Paul now?" I asked when we were out of earshot. "Do you still think he's a *tupapu*?"

"I don't know what I think he is," Tehane said. "Maybe he is a sly *tupapu*. Maybe he is a shy creature who comes to the edge of the fire and paints what he sees and hears. Maybe he is something else. I will cook him dinner tonight. I will eat with you both. But I will not trust him ever. And neither should you. That is what I think."

Not trust Paul? I just shook my head.

That night turned into a bigger party than I'd planned on. Tehane invited Anani and his family, her mama, Kwok, and some people I hardly even knew. All in all, we had more than a dozen. The wood I'd chopped went to build a big fire on the beach. We roasted the fish over it, together with some bananas. Anani brought a ham. Kwok brought three bottles of wine. Paul brought himself and his sketchbook.

We ate and drank, and Paul ate and drank and drew. We kept him hopping that night. He'd gobble some food, then pick up the wine and swig it out of the bottle. Then he'd see something and put down the wine and start drawing.

The night kept on unfolding from one thing to the next until it felt as if the party were a frisky animal that we were all part of, and the night and fire and surf sounds were as alive as we were.

Anani and the other men started dancing the Tahitian hula. It's different from the Hawaiian kind. The Tahitians jump and stamp and thrust like some kind of war dance. Paul watched for a few minutes, then joined the line.

The others all laughed as Paul kicked up the sand and threw his arms around. He didn't get a single step right.

He fell out of the line and got his guitar. He tried playing along with the dancing but that didn't work either. So he just thumped the guitar in time with the music. Then he gave that up and started drinking again, wandering around hugging people.

Finally he stretched out on the grass and toasted the sky.

"I love you all," he shouted. "I will be one of you."

Kwok cocked an eye at me. I knew it meant, "Including me?" Then he stretched and wished us all good night.

With Kwok gone, the party changed. Anapa and some of the other kids lay down to sleep by the fire. After a while, the grown-ups started to join them. Even the moon went down.

Tehane went around picking up the bits of trash and putting them into a crate. I banked the fire. We were the last ones up.

I felt proud of us. We had made this night. Friends were sleeping around the fire I had made, full of the food Tehane had helped fix. I looked over at her bent over to pick up a pork bone and decided she was about perfect.

All of a sudden Paul stood up and motioned to me. His face looked grim and pale under the stars.

I went over to him, and he slung an arm across my shoulders. "Totefa," he gasped. "Totefa, my good angel. From Los Angeles, the City of Angels. Are there many angels there, Totefa? Are there as many angels there as there are here?"

Then he went slack and fell to his knees. His body shook.

"Damn," he said when the fit or whatever it was had passed. "I am getting old. When I was a sailor, a night like this would have been nothing to me. But what sailor ever had such a night?"

Tehane came over to us. She looked scared, but ready to do whatever needed to be done. I loved her more than ever then.

"Help me stand him up," I said.

The two of us got Paul on his feet. "I only want to be worthy of you, my savage angels," he said. "I want to be worthy of this place." Then he sagged his head over onto Tehane's breast.

"I am alone," he said. "I want to go home."

"You are home, Paul," I said to cheer him up.

He turned his face to me.

"*Siempre vais acercantándome las mercedes,*" he whispered.

It was something I'd heard Abuelita say. "You're always bringing me more mercies" was the closest thing to it in English, but that wasn't very close.

He dropped his arms.

"I am better now," he said. "Good night, my angels."

He moved a few steps, picked up his beret, and started for home.

"Want me to go with you?" I called after him.

But he didn't answer, and the dark took him in.

Tehane and I lay down together on the beach. I was worried about Paul, but the sound of the waves began to work on me and put me to sleep.

"Wonder what the matter with him is?" I said. "He acted drunk, but I think it was more than that."

"I wonder what is wrong with him too," Tehane said. "But you're right. It isn't wine. It is something worse."

Then I sat up.

"Paul forgot his sketchbook," I said.

Tehane pulled me down beside her.

"Don't worry," she said. "He will be back for it."

CHAPTER THIRTEEN

Titi Again

Two days after the party, Titi came in on the mail coach.

"Hello, Joe," she called out when she saw me. "Are you surprised to see me again?"

"Yep," I said. "I sure didn't figure on you leaving Papeete for someplace smaller."

"Love makes us do strange things," she said. "Carry my trunk over to Monsieur Gauguin's for me, sweetheart. It's too heavy for me."

"Huh?" I said. But I picked up the trunk. If Titi was moving in with Paul, he must want her here.

He was standing in his doorway when we got there, watching for her. He came across the yard and took her in his arms and kissed her.

"Here we live and be happy," he said in Tahitian.

"Whatever you say," she said.

I set down the trunk.

"Totefa, this is Titi," Paul said.

"We've met," I said. "Back in Papeete."

"Then you will already know how delightful she is," Paul said.

"Sure thing," I agreed.

"I want to give a party," Paul said. "I have had a little money from France, and I want to celebrate Titi's coming. Will you and Mademoiselle Tehane come this Saturday night?"

"I'll come for sure," I told him. "I can't say about Tehane."

Suddenly, I was anxious to be gone. There was something really wrong with this. It had a little of that old Smoking Mirror feeling, only for Paul instead of me. "Well, I'd better go see what Anani wants me for today."

And I left them there.

I was pretty sure Paul didn't love Titi. And I was even surer Titi didn't love anybody but herself. So why had Paul asked her to come? He kept talking about how beautiful the primitive was, and how pure savage things were. Titi was about as savage and primitive as one of Kwok's cola drinks. He must be mighty lonely. But if he was happy with her, I reckoned that was what mattered.

Tehane didn't exactly agree when I told her a day later.

"That man is a fool," she said. "A girl like that Titi will never make him happy. He is pretending she is something she is not and doesn't want to be. He is always pretending things are what they are not. I think you should stay away from him."

"I'm going to that party," I said. "Are you coming or not?"

"If you are going, I suppose I must," Tehane said.

When Saturday night came, Tehane and I showed up just after dark.

All the oil lamps were burning inside Paul's house, and he'd pushed as many things out of the way as he could to make more

room. I saw a new painting hanging on the wall, along with the
himene picture and the one of Aori. It was so new, you could smell
the paint.

Sitting on a low stool right beside it was Jénot, with one of Paul's
cups in his hand. Anani and Tehura were there too. Tehane and I and
Paul and Titi made up the rest of the party. I could tell they'd all started drinking a while ago.

Paul greeted me with an *abrazo,* a hug like Spaniards give one
another. He was wearing his beret, a white shirt with an orchid lei
over it, and a tapa cloth *pareo* around his waist. Titi has in a nice dress
that must have come from Europe or the States.

"*Ia orana,* Totefa. *Ia orana,* Mademoiselle Tehane," Paul said.
"Good, we are all here now. I must introduce everyone. Mademoiselle Tehane, my friend Lieutenant Jénot of the Papeete garrison.
Mademoiselle Titi. Jénot, this is Totefa Sloan, of whom we were
speaking earlier."

Jénot got up and offered his hand.

"I am glad to see you again," he said. "I still recall our last conversation."

"So do I," I said. "He was here one day a few weeks ago. But he
left right away."

"Kwok told me," Jénot said. "He has been absent from these
waters since. Perhaps he is travelling farther afield to find new natives
to cheat."

"Likely so," I agreed. Then to change the subject I said, "I like the
new painting, Paul."

"A development of the theme of the first one," Paul said. "And I have two more much like it in preparation. But always so far I am painting things seen at a distance. When will these good people allow me to come close and paint them?"

He turned to Tehane.

"*Mademoiselle*, I have asked you before. I ask now. Would you consent to be painted?"

Before she could answer, Titi laughed. "He wants to paint you in the altogether. I told him he should only paint me like that, but he says I am too—what is the word you used, Paul?"

"Civilized," Paul said with his jaw tight.

"I'm very civilized." Titi laughed. "I love everything civilized. Clothes, money, and shopping. Why don't we go to Papeete for shopping, love?"

"Perhaps civilized was not quite the right word," Paul said to Titi. "Perhaps deracinated, cut off from your own roots. Perhaps there are better words for why I choose not to paint you."

I didn't think Paul and Titi were getting along as well as he'd hoped.

"I am also too civilized," Tehane said. "Thank you, Monsieur Gauguin."

"I assure you, *mademoiselle*, I had no such thought," Paul said. "I had no such thought. I thought perhaps a painting of you and Totefa."

Tehane shook her head.

"Well, I'm game," I said. "You can paint me if you want."

"You can't paint her," Titi went on. "She's part French. She's as de-what-you-said as I am."

"No," Paul said. "She has purity. The purity you lack."

Titi laughed. "Purity!"

And Tehane blushed. I was beginning to wish we hadn't come to this party.

But now it was time to eat. Paul had put out a spread of the best from Kwok's store. There were canned tomatoes and bottled candied fruit and a big lump of tinned meat. To this he'd added bananas and breadfruit and some flowers.

"Be seated, everyone," Paul commanded, and filled his glass. Then he realized he'd never offered Tehane and me anything to drink and splashed some wine into a couple more of his goblets.

"To my dear companion, Titi," He toasted. "May our lives together be long and happy."

So we all raised our glasses. But Tehane didn't drink.

"So you do not drink to me and Paul," Titi said. "Why?"

"I do not drink." Tehane smiled.

"You're very rude," Titi said. "Not civilized."

That made me mad.

"Excuse me, Titi. I think you'd better apologize for that," I said in English.

"She should apologize, not me," Titi said.

"Apologize, Titi," Paul roared.

She threw her drink in his face.

It got very quiet at that table. The loudest sound was a drop of wine falling off Paul's cheek and hitting the floor. He tilted back his head and looked at Titi from under his heavy-lidded eyes. Then, without changing expression, he caught her with a roundhouse swing that made her head crack.

A blow like that would have decked me, but Titi was big. She shook her head and leaped at Paul, and they both went over onto the floor, punching and shouting.

Jénot and Anani and I got them separated before they killed each other.

When the two of them were standing on opposite sides of the room where we'd dragged them, Jénot holding Paul and Anani and me holding Titi, Tehura said, "My husband, it is time we went home."

"You going to behave yourself, Titi?" I asked in English.

"Yes. Go. The party's over," she said.

"I'd say you're about right," I agreed, and took my hands off her.

Tehane stood up and took my arm.

"Take me home," she said.

"Night, Paul," I said, as we went out the door. "Night, lieutenant."

No one answered.

Tehane and I walked to her home under a crescent moon that came and went through sky islands of clouds. For a long time neither of us said anything.

Finally I said, "Well, you were right."

"I take no pleasure in it," Tehane said.

After another long time, I said, "Maybe you're right about Paul too. I don't know. But I can't help liking the guy."

"You love him," she said. "You love him as you did Robert."

I shook my head.

"It's different," I said. "I understood Robert." Then I said, "Sure you don't want to come back to my place?"

"Not tonight," she said. "Come to see me tomorrow."

We kissed good night when we reached her place. The little light was on inside to keep away the *tupapus*. The dog gave a friendly bark.

"Okay, tomorrow then," I said.

I took it slow and easy back to my shack. I walked down to the beach and let the waves soothe away the feelings from the party. When they finally did, I turned for home. I rolled into my hammock and fell asleep.

It was past midnight when a soft pounding on the door woke me.

"Tehane?" I said, hoping.

"Paul," said a voice.

When I opened my door, he was standing there with an old sea bag beside him.

"I need a place to stay," he said. "Just for tonight."

I let him in. He slung his hammock in the corner opposite mine, and we both lay quietly in the dark for a while.

"Totefa, my ever-generous savage. Why is it I cannot, by my best efforts, be what you are without trying?" Paul said.

I didn't have anything to say to that, so I just lay there.

The moon had crossed my window and gone down for the night when he started to cry.

CHAPTER FOURTEEN

Tehura Poses

It struck me as strange that Paul and Titi didn't split up after that night, but they didn't. He went back the next day, and they lived together for weeks.

Things didn't get any better for them though. Their fights could be heard all over Mataiea. And there were other fights, between Titi and Tehura. Tehura didn't like Titi always chasing off her boys when they played around Paul's place. They'd always done it, and she saw no reason why they should stop just because an artist had moved into the old house and was trying to paint. Who needed art anyway?

Things came to a head when Tehura hung out some laundry, and later, when she went to bring it in, her white cotton dress was missing.

I was helping to patch the thatch on the old place the day that happened, so I had a good view from up on the roof.

It was Titi who came to answer her knock.

"Did you take my white dress?" Tehura asked.

"I didn't know you had a white dress," Titi said. "Anyway, why would I want it? My clothes are much nicer than yours. I get them in Papeete."

Tehura wore that white dress at least once a week. Titi must have seen it.

"Where is Monsieur Gauguin?" Tehura asked.

"Out drawing someplace, I suppose," Titi said. "I don't know."

This was another lie. Paul was out behind the house with his easel set up, not fifty yards away. When the two women started shouting at each other, he came around the front to see what the trouble was.

"Monsieur Gauguin, I think your Titi has stolen my white dress," Tehura said. "I want you to help me look for it."

"No! She can't come in!" shouted Titi.

"*Madame,* I do not know if Titi has stolen your dress or not," Paul said. "But I know it would not be beneath her. Come, let us search her things."

Sure enough, Tehura found her dress in Titi's trunk, while Titi screamed at her and Paul and called them both every name she knew in three languages.

Tehura came out again with her dress under her arm and rounded on Paul.

"Monsieur Gauguin, my husband likes you, but I do not," she said. "I like Titi even less. You had better find another place to live."

"*Madame,* it is Titi who must find another place," Paul said. "I am finished with her."

What Titi said next everybody in Mataiea heard, and she went on for a long time. Paul spent the night at my place.

The next day Titi was packed and on the mail coach back to Papeete.

So Paul could stay. Anani wanted him to. He liked Paul and liked having the artist living in one of his houses. But Tehura still wanted him gone. Paul tried to offer the peace pipe. He had the idea of painting Tehura's picture in her white dress. Again, Anani liked the idea and Tehura didn't. But he talked her into it, and Tehura became the first person in Mataiea ever to sit for a painting.

Paul worked hard on it and finished it in a few days. Then he invited me and Tehane over to come and see it, even before Anani and Tehura. But I went alone. Tehane was still angry about the party and didn't want to see Paul.

I was surprised when I saw it. I was in the picture. Or anyway, I guessed it was me. I was at the back, riding a little brown pony and wearing my Stetson and looking into the house. If I'd really been there, I'd have been looking at Tehura's back. He put Tehane's dog in the doorway looking at me. But the important part of the painting was Tehura. She was sitting on the floor with her legs crossed and her face turned away and resting on her hand, as if she hadn't wanted to look at Paul.

"Why did you put me in it?" I asked.

"Take a look at that woman," Paul said. "Imagine what it was like being in the same room with that face, knowing how she felt. I put you into the picture to have something joyful."

"You think I'm joyful?" I said.

"You are a symbol of joy, life, freedom, truth in this painting," Paul said.

"What about the dog?" I said. "Is he a joyful spirit too?"

"The dog is Tehura's spirit, on guard against what you represent," Paul said.

Well, it was a good painting. Looking at it, I could feel the heat on my skin and the strength of the pony under me. And he had Tehura's face down perfectly. For the first time I understood that paintings didn't have to look like photographs to be true. But still, I hadn't been there. And neither had the dog.

I said something about it.

"Totefa, you sound like an Impressionist," Paul laughed.

"A what?" I asked.

"A group of artists in France," he said. "Friends of mine, some of them. When I had money, I used to buy their work. I was almost one of them for a while. They would agree with you. Their whole belief was to paint what was in front of them, and how they reacted to it. Their impressions. But what does that tell us about the reality of anything?"

"A lot?" I said.

"A lot perhaps, but not enough," Paul said. "We savages do not make art to show us merely what a thing is. We make art to show us what things mean."

"Well anyway, I'm proud to be in it," I said.

"Good," Paul said. "Because, friend, I had another reason for putting you in the painting. I wanted to see if I could paint some part of the truth of you. Just a little to see if I was ready. I think I can say that I am. I would like to paint you again in more depth. Will you agree?"

"Sure," I said.

"And perhaps Mademoiselle Tehane as well?" he said. "Wearing that lovely blue-and-white dress she wore on that disastrous night when I tried to welcome Titi into my life here."

"Don't count on that," I said. "Tehane's just not interested in being in your paintings."

Paul sighed.

Paul showed his work to Anani and Tehura next, and he liked the painting and she didn't. Said she wouldn't have it in the house. So Paul took it and set it up for sale in the vacant lot next to Kwok's store.

Everyone in Mataiea saw it. And no one in Mataiea had ever seen anything like it. It amazed them that someone could make a picture of someone they knew. People stood around the painting all day, talking about it and asking one another why Tehura looked so angry and was the little man in the back really me when I didn't have a pony? It was talk story for two days afterward; and because of it, people began to agree to let Paul paint them. So he got something he wanted, even though no one offered so much as a red banana to buy it.

Tehura didn't like what Paul had done though, and this time Paul was out of that house, no ifs, ands, buts, or maybes.

When I heard that he was going to be turned out, it made me remember how I'd felt losing our ranch. That was no way for anybody to feel. So I went to Anani and asked if I could take in Paul.

Anani said, "Yes. He will not be around here anymore, and that will suit you, won't it, my wife?"

"It will suit me as long as he never comes to the house," Tehura said. "You will still be welcome, Totefa, but never he."

When I told him, Paul wrung my hand.

"I accept, Totefa. I will be very happy to live with you. I only hope I can be a worthy friend."

So that day we started moving his things down to my place. There wasn't nearly as much stuff as there had been when he came from Papeete. Some of the furniture was gone, and so were the fishing tackle and all of the instruments except the guitar. A lot of the cases of food were used up, and there was a lot less of paint than there had been. Even so, my place was small; and once we'd got everything in, we had just enough room to turn around in.

Some things Paul'd kept. He still had his swords and shotgun, and of course his art was everywhere. His cups and vases were sitting on the windows and even wedged into gaps in the walls. We hung a few from the rafters just because we didn't have any other place to put them.

His paintings were stacked up against the wall beside the door. His canvas rolls and paints made a mountain that took up a quarter of the floor. His potter's wheel was in one corner, and his easel was in another. That left two for our hammocks. When time came to put up the little friends, we covered the walls with them wherever we could find room.

"You know, I feel as if I'm living in a painting now," I said as we finished. "A whole lot of paintings."

"I hope you may always feel that way, Totefa," he said. "As for me, I feel I am truly myself at last. This is rich. Rich."

He sat down in the doorway that faced the sea. The late sun was turning the lagoon as bright as a mirror in places.

"I had another friend in France," he said. "Another artist. He invited me to live with him too. It was a long way from Paris, but I thought we might be able to do great things together. I believed he had something to teach me about art. Because he was a genius. And I suppose he did, in a way. I tried to paint like him and found that I could not. Only Vincent could paint like Vincent. And that was when I finally knew that only I could paint the images waiting to be born in me. The pictures in my savage blood."

"Did Vincent mind much when you came here?" I asked.

"I had to leave," Paul said. "He went mad and took to following me around. One night I came home to find he'd tried to cut off his ear."

"Why?" I gasped.

"Why do the mad do anything?" Paul said. "I came home and the *gendarmes* were there, and there was blood all over his room. You, Totefa, you are greater than Vincent." He went on. "You offer me shelter not from your need but from mine. And from your own great heart. It is this that everyone loves in you."

"I'm going to run off if you go talking like that," I said.

"Enough then," he said. "I am hungry. What shall we do about dinner?"

That was the first time I realized having Paul in the house might be a problem.

"Well, Paul, Tehane kind of expects me over at her place for dinner most nights," I said.

"Ah," he said. "Then I shall dine alone. Very well."

"I guess I'd better clean up and get over there," I said.

"Your stove is a simple thing. I will have no difficulty with it," Paul said.

"Just help yourself," I said.

I didn't feel right leaving him behind like that. I knew there wasn't much food in the house. But I couldn't just show up on the doorstep with an extra mouth either.

So I washed up quickly and started over to Tehane's place. Maybe, I thought, when she heard Paul and I were living together, she'd just say to bring him along when I came.

CHAPTER FIFTEEN

Shipmates

That was not what she said.

Tehane was furious when I told her what I'd done. She smouldered all through dinner; and as soon as it was over, she hauled me outside away from the house and lit into me.

"What did you invite him to live with you for?" she shouted at me. "I can't come and visit you at night while he lives there."

I stopped to think that over.

"Damn," I said.

I thought some more.

"Damn," I said.

"Now you think of these things," Tehane snapped.

"But, Tehane, I couldn't do anything else," I said. "He needed a place. And I'm the only one who could give him one."

"He is not a good man," she said.

"You can't say that," I said. "He's never done you any harm. He's never hurt anybody."

"He thinks I am a savage," she said.

"He thinks *I* am a savage. He wishes he was a savage. That's his compliment. Heck, Tehane, he likes you."

"Oh, he likes me very well," Tehane said. "He looks at me as if he wants to eat me. Have you never seen it? That man is living in some dream he has made about this place. And it is a bad dream, however well he paints it. It is not true. He looks at you and me and lies to himself and tries to live his lies. We are not real to him."

"They're not lies," I said. "They're stories. Sure, he makes up things sometimes, but he knows he's doing it. And maybe he does look at you; but, Tehane—you're beautiful."

"Who do you love, him or me?" she asked.

"That's crazy to say," I said. "You know I love you."

"But you want to live with him."

"But you don't want to live with me," I said. "You said so."

"I will not live with you, but I love you," she said.

She turned away and walked over to a palm tree and stood under it, with her arms crossed over her breasts. Finally she said, "Do you want to marry me or not?"

"Well," I said after a while. "I was planning to ask you. Sometime."

"When?" she said.

"I hadn't quite decided," I said.

"I think you had better decide. Very soon," Tehane said.

My head was running off in six different directions at once. Did I love Tehane? Yes, I did. Was I ready to marry her? Maybe, maybe not. Did I want her to leave me because I wasn't ready to marry her? No, I did not. But I realized that I'd never thought of staying in

Tahiti forever. In my mind, I'd always sort of thought I'd ship out again or go back to the States. And how was I supposed to keep a wife?

But there was something else. Who was Tehane to say I couldn't help out Paul? Paul, who'd done as much for me as Tehane had in his way.

"I've got to go," I said. "I've got to think."

"Good. It is time you started," Tehane said.

And she ran into her house.

I just stood there for a while. Then I went down to the beach and the sound of the surf.

It was another of those nights when the clouds came and went like ghost ships before the moon, stealing the light and giving it back, turning the sea silver and black.

Old Smoking Mirror was at me again. It was clear enough that Tehane was laying down the law to me about Paul, and about us. Once more my life was being broken up.

"Damn," I said to myself over and over again. "Damn, damn, damn."

After a long time it came to me like this: Tehane might be right about Paul, but I was right too. She couldn't see what was in him the way I could, because he didn't show her that side of himself. He didn't share that with anybody but me. But that was the real man, the one who'd seen into me and seen his own best self shining back. Or at any rate he thought he had. And right now he needed me, maybe more than Tehane did. Maybe I was wrong, but that was what I saw in the flickering waves and heard in their voices that night.

I didn't know what Smoking Mirror had in mind, but I knew

what I had to do. I went home, to the little dark cabin where Paul was sleeping.

I tiptoed in and rolled into my hammock. I could hear Paul's deep breathing in the other corner. I looked at the things all around the room catching the little stripes of light that came in through the spaces in the walls. The strange-faced cups and vases. The little friends.

What was it about art that made it so important to Paul? So important that he'd given up his family and moved halfway around the world to give himself to his ideas? And could I even understand it if he tried to explain it to me? I didn't know. But lying there already missing Tehane, I felt a little as if I were shipping out again, just as I'd always thought I would. Paul was the captain; I was the crew. Maybe he didn't know where he was going, maybe he did. But I could feel the wind blowing into the shack, stirring up things. We were on our way somewhere. Shipmates.

CHAPTER SIXTEEN

Rosewood

Paul started turning out a lot of stuff after he moved in. He was always at his easel, or at his wheel, throwing a pot. For relaxation he'd carve another cup or woodcut. During that time I never saw him without a brush, knife, or lump of clay in his hand unless he was eating or sleeping.

"I am doing at last the work that is in my blood, Totefa," he said. "My blood speaks to me at night when I sleep, and in the morning I must serve it. You have given me this. I will never be able to repay you, but I will give you back what I can. You will live in my paintings and it may be that one day you will be as famous as Olympia. It is all I can give you."

"I'm just glad to see you working so much, Paul," I told him. "The way you're turning out things, pretty soon you'll have a whole bunch of stuff to send back to France. I'll bet if you only sell half of it you'll be able to get all your gear back from Kwok."

Paul only laughed and went on painting.

He started to paint some of the *vahinés,* girls who'd seen the painting of Tehura and liked it; but he never painted any man but me. He put me in four of five paintings after that first one, always in the foreground somewhere. The thing was though, the more he painted me the less it looked like me.

In the first painting I was leading a white horse, a real beauty. I would have loved to have ridden it, but it didn't exist. It was just copied from one of the little friends. He put me into a *pareo* cloth, too, instead of my jeans. There was a girl coming toward me through the trees. She wasn't anybody, so Paul didn't give her a face. He put Tehane's best blue-and-white dress on her though. He called it *The Rendezvous*.

He made me look taller and handsomer than I really was too.

"I must paint you as you really are, Totefa," he said. "Not as you look."

And the more he praised me and relied on me for things, the better I liked myself. We were shipmates, like I'd been with Robert.

When I wasn't working for Anani or Kwok, I'd help Paul stretch canvas or sharpen his knives. I did the cooking too, which was mostly bananas and breadfruit and what fish I could catch. I even helped him work out how to make a paste from breadfruit that he could smear on his canvases as a base for paint when he started to run out of white.

When it was too dark to work anymore, we'd sit outside our place, either facing Aori or watching the sea, and we'd talk. Mostly Paul talked and I listened. He went on about everything: his memories of Peru, his kids, his wife, how much money he'd made when he was working in the stock market, his cruises to Brazil with the

French merchant marine. But he always came back to art. He threw out a lot of names of other artists he'd known. He talked real respectfully of his teacher, a fellow named Pissarro, and a whole lot less respectfully of Degas and Seurat, who sounded like a couple of dudes.

That was the good part of our lives. The bad part was money. I didn't get much, and with Paul there, there wasn't enough. I don't say he didn't do what he could. His pile of things got smaller and smaller as I took them over to Kwok to trade for things he needed; and I knew if he'd made any money, he'd have shared it with me. But there never was any.

Every couple of weeks he'd get letters from France or from his wife in Denmark, and he'd tear them open and read them with a fierce look. But the news was always the same. There'd been this or that said about his work, or maybe a mention in a magazine. But nobody wanted to buy what he was sending home.

Some of the time the mail came with Lieutenant Jénot. He liked to visit Paul when he could get away from Papeete. He usually left a little money for Paul behind when he went. Sometimes it was a loan, sometimes it wasn't. Jénot was the best.

When he ran out of heavy canvas, I came up with an idea to keep Paul working. I asked Kwok for some old burlap sacks. We stretched them, smeared some of our homemade gesso on them, and they worked pretty well. The burlap showed through in some places, but Paul said he liked the look.

"Rough," he said. "Real. Another step beyond Impressionism. Once again, Totefa, I am in your debt."

As for me, I missed Tehane. I saw her all the time, but always at a distance, as if she were in one of Paul's early paintings. And every time I did, my heart would jump, I wanted to be with her so bad. But she would turn away when she saw me, and I would turn away when she did.

One day when I came home from cutting wood, I saw Paul out in the yard, waving one of his swords around. He was slashing the air and dancing back and forth through the sand as if there were a whole army of art critics in front of him, and the look on his face told me he meant business.

Scattered around him were some of the little wooden heads he'd been carving.

I just watched him until he finally stopped for breath.

"I'm no longer good even at this," he said when he saw me. "Do you know, I used to be a truly dangerous man with a blade? Fencing was the only subject I was good at in school. But I'm getting old. Old and slow. Damn it."

"What happened?" I asked. "Bad news from France?"

He waved his hand.

"No. That I would have expected. What I did not foresee was that this island itself would betray me. Look at this."

He tossed one of the heads to me. I saw that it had begun to rot.

"This foul, soft wood of the tropics," he said. "So easy to work and so quick to die. These things are my destiny, Totefa. To rot in these islands and be forgotten."

I'd never heard Paul so angry-sad before.

"I am a lost man," he said. "I am an artist, a great artist. I know this. And because I know it, I endure. I endure the stupidity of the art world and the endless loneliness of being apart from my fellow men. From my family. Poverty. I suffer all this because I know that what is in me is in no one else and will die silent and unknown if I do not release it. But by God, when art itself turns on me! Totefa, I have nothing in this world but my art."

He sat down in the sand surrounded by his little heads. He looked completely whipped.

"There are rosewood trees up on Aori," I said, holding the little carving in my hands. "Rosewood's tough."

Paul looked at the sand and the little figures lying in it for a long time. Then he said, "Yes. I could do good work in rosewood."

We started off early the next morning with a couple of axes I'd borrowed from Anani. I'd never climbed Aori before; but there were clear trails lower down, and I figured we could get up to where the rosewood grew on the high, cool slopes, cut what we needed, and get back down by dark. Anyway, Paul thought so well of me, I wanted to do something to prove he was right. Going up on that mountain to find him something he needed was a kind of test for me.

It was a long, hard climb. Aori was steep and stony. The trail we were on narrowed down to a zigzag that doubled back on itself a hundred times, and we had to walk one behind the other.

Finally the trail dead-ended at a whitewater stream, and we had to climb along that. We went up one side, then the other, then the first one again, wherever there was a little clear space to walk on.

Crossing, it was hard work not to lose our feet as the water rushed against us, and it wasn't long before Paul started breathing hard. Sometimes the water would pool at the foot of a little fall and we'd see eels swimming around, looking at us as if they wondered who we thought we were to disturb them.

The stream had cut a deep, narrow canyon, and sometimes it was so dark in it that when I looked up, I could see the stars. That water was cold too, and sometimes a wind would blow down on us from higher up. I began to shiver in the middle of the hot tropical day.

The weight of our axes began to drag on us. Paul kept lagging farther and farther back. I had to slow down for him. Then we came to a place where the brush and vines grew so thick that we had to climb through them with our feet not even touching the ground. I began to wonder if this had been such a good idea.

Finally we pushed through the last of the thicket and came out to a place where Aori threw out a big shoulder to our left, and growing there we saw a stand of trees.

I didn't have the breath to do anything but point.

We reached the grove, and Paul strutted among those trees, looking them over as if he were buying a horse. Finally he slapped a trunk with his palm and said, "This one, Totefa. This one is mine."

"We could rest awhile before we cut it down," I said.

Paul didn't answer me. There was a look on his face that a man might have if he'd just found a gold mine. Fierce, greedy, and full of joy. "You shall not die, but change," he told the tree, and crossed himself.

He took his ax and swung, cutting a deep notch.

Well, he was tireder than I was. I took the other side and matched his strokes. We had the tree down in less than half an hour. Paul cut off one of the big branches, a piece almost too big for both of us to lift. We trimmed it, and then, finally, we rested.

We were so high up that a few small clouds were drifting below us and we could look at their tops. The sun looked as if it were just beyond our reach. We could see all the way back to Mataiea.

I was hungry, but too tired to want to go looking for fruit. I just wanted to lie there in the sun and be glad we had found what we'd come for.

Paul was lying beside me with his hands behind his head and his eyes closed. Without opening them, he started to talk.

"Did you ever make a voyage to New Zealand, Totefa?" he asked me.

"No. Australia once," I told him.

"They say that the Maoris there carve the most elaborate and fantastic things," he said. "They say the art of these island people reaches its apex there. That what they make is like nothing else on earth. You see no such carvings here in Tahiti. Why? They are the same people; it is the same language. But where is their art?"

"They tell long stories and they sing real good," I said. "Maybe that's their art."

I didn't see why anybody had to run up a bunch of statues and things just so he could look at them. Words and music were enough for them, and for me, too.

"Like the Vikings, and the ancient Irish," Paul said. "It may be so." He paused. "Yesterday in my despair I saw only that I was poor and destined to be forgotten," he continued. "But now I think I was sent here to create the art of this place for all the world to see."

"Who sent you? God?" I asked.

"Perhaps," Paul said. "Whatever God may be. Whatever deep-voiced Thing spoke the word that first created and then created us to go on creating everything that lies in the dark and silence, waiting to be born."

He stood up and threw his arms at the sky. "I have cut away the last of my old life," he shouted. "I will no longer worry about money, or my reputation in Paris. All that is cut out of me as we cut this tree."

He looked like a tree to me, standing there that way. But I noticed how long his shadow was.

"You ready to start back?" I said. "Getting this log down's going to be a job and a half."

"Yes," Paul said. "I am ready for anything now."

CHAPTER SEVENTEEN

Matamoe

Paul really was different after that day. He sold practically everything he had left of what he'd brought with him, even the shotgun.
About the only things he kept were his swords and his art gear, and
one good suit for when he went back to France someday. Kwok took
nearly everything else, trading most of it for food and wine.

Then Paul sent word all over Mataiea that he was throwing a
party on the next Friday night. He even invited Kwok and Minot and
sent a message to his friend Jénot.

Paul had mixed big piles of Tahitian foods with special cakes and
candies, and had a barrel of beer set out on cloths under the trees.
And there was a roast pig that we'd cooked all day.

When everything was ready, Paul dressed up. He took off his
French clothes and wrapped a *pareo* cloth around his waist. Then he
put on his beret. Last, he put a tiare behind his ear, as if he was a
married woman.

"You know, Paul," I said to him when he put it on, "folks might
laugh, the way they did when you got off the boat in Papeete."

"I am marrying this island," he said. "I am married to it. Let anyone laugh who wishes. I am Paul Gauguin."

People started coming at sunset, bringing flowers, more food, and their songs. We lit torches when it got dark and built a big fire. By dark the yard behind our place was packed. Almost everyone in town was there except Kwok and Minot. And Tehane and her family.

Paul kept moving through the crowd, shaking hands, bowing, saying "*Ia orana*" to everybody. Nobody laughed at his flower, but he laughed. He laughed a lot that night; and every laugh rang out deep as a wave against the reef, and there was no bitterness in any of them. When the men started dancing, he joined in; and though he couldn't follow their movements, he stomped the sand and threw his arms around in a dance of his own, and the people watching beat time for him with their hands.

Finally he stopped trying and made up a dance of his own. The rest of us watched. He jumped as if he were trying to catch the moon. He stalked the ocean waves and danced backward as they chased him up the beach. He spun until his beret fell off and went flying like a lonely little *tupapu*.

"Who is this man?" Tehura asked me. "This is not the same fellow who came to Mataiea with trunks and suitcases."

"I don't always understand Paul," I said. "But maybe that's not important." Then I joined the dancing myself, feeling good that maybe Tehura was liking Paul for the first time.

Jénot was there, enjoying himself like a kid. Away from Papeete, he could afford to let down; and he sure did that night. He was acting silly with a tiare in his teeth, showing some little kids how they ballet dance in France, jumping around and twisting his leg out behind him in what he called an arabesque.

After a long time Paul got everyone's attention by banging on a big pot lid with a stick.

"*Ia orana,*" he shouted.

"*IA ORANA,*" the crowd roared back.

Then he tried to make a speech in Tahitian.

"Friends of Mataiea. My good friends. I come here some time back, and I were strange to you. I love you, but you do not know that. And I cannot show you because I do not know how. I am still a Frenchman inside too much. But soon—I mean, not long back now—I find my way to be more honest. More free. More savage. Now I can show love. This party makes me free. Now I poor as any Tahitian. Now I no longer worry about French things. I only live like you and work. Thank you for be my neighbors."

People cheered. People clapped. A lot of the men hugged Paul. He wasn't a little guy; but when those Tahitians wrapped their arms around him, he about disappeared. But the smile never left his face.

At the end, when people were falling asleep in the yard or going back to their homes, Tehura came over to him.

"Monsieur Gauguin, if you would care to move back into our old house, you may do so for free," she said.

Paul bowed. "Thank you, *madame,* but if my friend Totefa can tolerate me, I prefer to remain here."

"*Santos,* Paul, you know you can stay," I said. "Aren't we shipmates?"

He hugged me and said. "You are my true friend, the picture of my best self. God help me if I ever forget that."

The painting Paul did of our day on Aori came a few days later. This time, he made me look Greek. He'd used the faceless statue as a model for me, put a *pareo* cloth on me, and made me taller; but it was me. There I was, chopping the rosewood.

He'd set me in front of our place, with a fire going and a couple of women in the background who were walking away. A little puff of white smoke was rising from a fire beside me. The sky was purple, the grass was yellow and green, and the bare ground was red-brown. The trees were different greens. But they didn't just lie there on the canvas. They swooped and swirled like dancing or like smoke.

"I call it *Matamoe*," Paul said.

"What does that mean?" I asked.

"What do you think it sounds like?" Paul smiled, looking at me from under his heavy-lidded eyes.

"It sounds a little like the Spanish for 'he kills,'" I said. "*Mata*. But I guess it must be some Tahitian word I don't know, because that *moe* throws me."

He threw back his head and laughed that free laugh I'd heard at the party.

"Totefa, you understand me so well! In fact, the title is a word game. *Mata* does indeed mean 'he kills.' But the second part is the French *moi* misspelled. He kills me. The old, dead, me."

"You see, Totefa?" Paul said, waving his arm in swirls like the clouds in the painting. "You are chopping the dead wood to make the fire. The fire makes the wood live again in a new form. Nothing is ever really destroyed without something being born in its place."

Abuelita used to say something like that about Smoking Mirror, I remembered. Had Paul been reborn on that mountain? Would I be reborn? Into what?

I noticed there was one more detail in the painting, something I'd never seen in Mataiea. In the foreground Paul had painted a peacock and his hen.

"When did we get peacocks?" I asked.

"They are a symbol," Paul said. "In ancient times the peacock was the sign of the love of the soul, the completed soul. They are what happened to me up on that volcano."

"My *abuelita* used to say that those long tail feathers were bad luck," I said.

"So? Well, the Hindus say those feathers glisten with the eyes of God," Paul said.

"Well, I hope the Hindus are right and Abuelita was wrong," I said. "But she was usually right."

CHAPTER EIGHTEEN

Olympia

Paul went on painting, carving, making. I kept on with my work, and with wanting Tehane. More than once I started over that way, but I always turned back. I missed her like my arm, but I was right, and I knew it. And wasn't the proof of it the way Paul was now?

He had a new piece of work finished every few days, and it seemed as if the ideas never stopped coming. Sometimes he'd interrupt himself to sketch some new thing that he had just thought of, or take a break from painting by working on a piece of that rosewood we'd found.

And in the evenings we'd talk till we fell asleep. Except for my nights with Tehane, it was the best time I'd ever had in my life.

So when I came home one day and found him gone, I was a little surprised. It was easy enough to figure out why he was gone; he'd taken his easel and a box of paints. Gone to paint outside, which was not usual for him then. I waited awhile, then started dinner and figured he'd be home in time for it. When he wasn't, I began to wonder when he was coming, because he sure couldn't paint in the dark.

I lit a lamp and sat down to wait. All around me were the little friends, his carvings, pots, and pictures. I had the feeling they were all looking friendly at me. Maybe Olympia was saying, "I'm sure glad you're here to help out, Joe Sloan." And maybe Paul's daughter, Aline, was saying, "Thank you for being a friend to my papa." And maybe the broken bit of Greek statue was saying, "I'm glad he chose me to copy when he painted you." And the little heads were sort of rumbling together in a sound that was part song and part surf underneath everything else.

At last when Paul did come home, he had his paints but not his easel. There was something else missing too. His easy way. As soon as I saw him, I could tell he was in a foul temper. Bad news from France, I figured.

"I made dinner," I said.

Paul didn't say anything. He just looked at me as if he wanted to hit me, then he dropped his paints, slammed out of the shack, and went down toward the beach.

I thought about following him, then I decided I wouldn't. When he wanted to talk, he'd talk. One thing you could count on Paul for was talk.

But he didn't come back till late. Not until after I'd hit the sack. I wasn't asleep though. I was wide awake.

It had been seven different kinds of dull and lonely without Paul around that night. I hadn't liked it. It was too much like my life had been before he and Tehane had come into it. Before Robert, even. I'd almost forgotten what that felt like. Sad, and as if I didn't matter to anyone, not even myself. I wanted Paul to come back and bring some of his good, crazy talk with him before I went to sleep.

At last I heard his feet coming slow and heavy along the beach. The door opened, and he stood in the light of the moon, a dark shadow.

I decided I'd speak first.

"What is it, *compadre*?" I said.

"Nothing," he said. He spoke in French, not Spanish.

"Is it your wife? I asked. "Are your children all right?"

"Why do you ask about them?" Paul snapped. "What are they to you?"

"You're so sad," I said. "I guessed, I was afraid, it might be bad news about them."

"The news about my family is always bad," he said. "But fortunately I have heard nothing from that quarter."

"Are you hungry?" I asked.

"I have eaten," he said.

And that was all he said. He stumbled around in the dark, slinging his hammock and bumping into things. Normally he would have cursed the boxes and furniture for getting in his way, but not tonight.

When I heard the hammock creak under his weight, I thought maybe he'd say more about what was deviling him, but he didn't. His breathing changed, and I knew he was asleep.

Finally I went to sleep too. Paul was back, but those old feelings were still with me. I didn't much care if I woke up or not.

The next day my nose awoke me to the smell of breakfast cooking.

"Madame Anani has given us eggs," he said, still speaking French.

"And Kwok the Merciless has taken two of my sketches in trade for coffee and for some cheese that I believe must be three hundred years old. I am making omelettes for us."

This was the first time Paul had cooked anything since he'd moved in. Whatever had been wrong with him before, I guessed he was at least trying to cheer up.

"Thanks," I said, and got up.

I sat down at the little wood square we called a table. Paul finished the omelettes and brought them over. The omelette was good, though the coffee was thick as axle grease. I was glad to get it though. It had been a while since we'd had any in the house.

"How did you pass your day yesterday?" he asked me.

"Same as usual," I said. "How did your painting go?"

Paul stiffened.

"Difficult. Very difficult," he said.

So the trouble was with his painting. I figured he was having some kind of artist's problem I wouldn't understand.

"Maybe you'd like to take the day off," I said. "We could borrow an outrigger and go out in the lagoon. Get some fish."

Paul shook his head. "I cannot; I must not. I must finish what I started yesterday."

"Oh. Well. Okay," I said.

"Totefa," Paul said, looking at me from under his eyelids. "You must understand. I may wish to be like you at times, but I am not like you. I have your wildness but not your cheery ignorance. I am an artist, and I must do my art. There may be times the artist betrays the man."

I didn't know what he was talking about. But I did not like the sound of it.

I said, "Doesn't matter, Paul. We're still shipmates."

He stood up from the table with his food half eaten.

"I must go," he said. "I will feed myself tonight. Do not cook for me."

Then he grabbed up his paints and stopped at the door.

"I am a bastard, you know," he said, and was gone, hurrying up the beach to town.

I didn't know what to make of that. But all of a sudden I wasn't Totefa.

I decided to finish his coffee and eggs. Then I went out and looked at the sea. When I'd done that, I thought I might as well go over and see Kwok.

The sky was low that day, with the clouds piling up until they made a solid wall of gray, and the air was thick with a storm. There'd be rough weather by night for sure.

I went into the store. I saw the two sketches Paul had traded stuck up behind the counter. I saw they were what he called studies, practice for the picture of me and the peacocks. Paul's shotgun was nearby, hanging from the ceiling. There were other things that had been his once, here and there. It was like looking at his life in Mataiea.

When I came into the store, it was empty. Then I heard something familiar from the back, the sound of a gun being snapped together. Kwok came in carrying his dad's old rifle. He must have been cleaning it, I thought.

"*Bonjour,* cowboy," Kwok said.

"*Bonjour* yourself," I said. "Need anything done today?"

Kwok pursed his lips. Then he said, "You tied the last red rag in the usual spot, didn't you?"

That had been three days ago.

"Sure," I said. "Why?"

"Just making sure," Kwok said.

"Want me to tie up another one?" I asked.

"Do it," Kwok said. "I'll pay you again."

"I'll do it tonight," I said.

Kwok leaned forward across the counter and said, "And be extra careful nobody sees you."

I nodded, took the rag he gave me, and went out.

Kwok called me back.

"You're a good man, Totefa," he said. "Here, take the money now."

"You can pay me tomorrow," I said.

"Just take it," he said. "No reason to wait."

"I won't say no," I said. "Any particular reason?"

"I pay you not to ask questions," Kwok said, kind of snappishly.

"Well, I'll be careful," I said.

I went out and looked again at the sky. The clouds were kneaded into long rolls like waves. They made me think of the sea, and all of a sudden the throught came to me that maybe it was time to ship out again.

Things were changing, it looked like. Tehane and I were on the outs, Paul was different, and even Kwok didn't seem to be the way he had been. Maybe Smoking Mirror was back, working on all of us.

The water in the lagoon was dark. Beyond the reef it was darker.

What surprised me was that the idea didn't seem all that bad. If I wasn't going to wait for the *Mateata* to come back and I didn't have Tehane, the only reason for staying was Paul. And if he was going to be different toward me, why not find a ship?

I walked up and down with that one for a while, thinking hard. The more I thought about it, the better an idea it seemed. But only if Tehane really was through with me, and only if Paul really didn't want me around anymore.

There was only one way to find that out, and that was to talk to them. Maybe if Tehane knew I was leaving she'd be sorry and we'd be together again. Maybe if I just asked Paul what was going on, everything would be all right. If not I could leave for Papeete anytime I wanted.

I started for Tehane's house.

"It is good to see you again, Totefa," Maria said, and hugged me. "It has been far too long. Does this mean you want Tehane to come back to you?"

"That's what I came to see her about," I said. "Is she here?"

"She has gone away for several days now," Maria said. "She never says where she is going, but I know it is not to the school. She always goes in that direction." She pointed toward Papeete.

"There's not much out that way but your family *marae*," I said.

"Perhaps that is where she goes," Madame de Pouning said. "Though I cannot think why."

I supposed it was worth a try to go looking there.

"If she comes back would you please let her know I came to see her?" I asked.

"I will," Madame de Pouning said. "But I do not think she will come home before dark."

I walked along the coast road until I came to the place where it joined up with the trail to the *marae*. Someone had been that way not long ago. Some of the grass along it had been stepped on, and there were a couple of sloppy footprints. They looked too big to be Tehane's though, and I wondered who would be going out that way and why.

Then I came to a new trail. Someone had gone off to the left toward a little grove of wild oranges. I decided to follow the path.

I had only gone a few hundred yards when I heard Paul's voice. I couldn't hear the words, and I didn't hear any answer. Maybe he was talking to himself.

I stood on the trail, asking myself if I should bother him or not. I knew he wouldn't like being interrupted. But I really wanted to tell him what I was thinking about and hear what he said to it. Maybe this was a good time, maybe not. The only way to find out was to see. I decided I'd go up quietly, and if he wasn't alone I'd leave the way I'd come. If he was then I'd risk bothering him.

I came up as silent as an Indian to where Paul was sitting with his back to me. He was hard at work, not noticing anything but his painting and the model in front of him.

It was Tehane. She was wearing a tiare behind her ear and a necklace of shiny black stones. That was all. Paul had posed her like Olympia.

She didn't see me at first. Her eyes were looking far away, not really seeing anything.

Then she looked up, saw me, and gasped. But she didn't move.

The gasp made Paul turn.

I saw the cock of his head, the look from under the eyelids. The man I'd seen the first day in Papeete was back.

"What, are you jealous?" he said.

CHAPTER NINETEEN

Shotgun

I didn't speak. I just turned and went down the trail again.

Neither of them came after me.

I wasn't just angry. I wasn't just shocked. Everything I thought I'd known about both of them had just been turned inside out. And so had I.

I was hit so hard I didn't even pay attention to where I was going. When I reached the place where the trail joined the road, I turned wrong and started to Papeete. I went a couple of miles, I guess, before I realized I wasn't even going the right way.

Or was I? Maybe my feet had carried me in the right direction all by themselves. What did I need to go back to Mataiea for? Hell, I could be in Papeete that night, and sign on with the first ship that would have me. It didn't matter where. I didn't belong on the earth. A ship was the only place for me.

So I kept on walking.

The rain was starting now, warm and heavy. There was thunder in the clouds, and long scars of lightning came and went, slicing across the sky.

How far had I come? Maybe halfway. A long way, anyhow. I stopped to rest.

And standing there in the rain, almost blind from it, I thought of the one reason I had to go back to Mataiea. Kwok's red rag. He'd paid me, and I had to do it. And since I'd promised to be careful, I couldn't do it until after dark.

Angry at myself, at him, at Paul and Tehane, angry at the world, I went back, cursing every step of the way.

It was late afternoon when I reached town again. Mataeia looked deserted. It was siesta, and everything was battened down against the storm. Even Kwok's store looked as if it was closed. Coconuts were falling everywhere, and the wind was whistling an ugly song through the trees.

I decided the only place for me to go was back to my shack. If the rain had chased Paul in there, I'd throw him out.

But when I got there, the place was empty. Everything was just as it had been that morning, except that the wind had blown the shutters open. The rain was coming in, staining some of the little friends, ruining them. I laughed.

"Good ol' storm," I said.

I started packing my seabag. It didn't take long. Then I took my hat in my hands and looked at it. Should I take it or leave it behind? I didn't want it anymore. But I didn't want to leave it where Paul would see it either. I didn't want him to know I was hurt so bad I couldn't even wear it. I decided to take it and throw it overboard as soon as my next ship was clear of the reef. I stuck it in my bag and went out through the door on the seaward side.

Rocking out in the harbor was the *Mateata*. She was riding low in the water, as if she had a full hold or maybe a leak.

Kwok had said the White Wolf owed him money. He'd want to know that the ship was back.

I headed over to the store. It was still closed up.

"Open up, Kwok. I've got something you'll want to know," I shouted, banging on the doors.

When he didn't come, I tried again. Then again. When that didn't work, I decided to try around back. I pounded and pounded, but he didn't answer. Finally, just to be sure, I tried the knob. The door swung open.

"Kwok, wake up," I shouted. "The *Mateata*'s back. You always said you wanted to know if she came in."

The store was dark inside, but Kwok had left a lantern beside the door. I lit it and shone it around.

Kwok's little room had been torn apart. His drawers had been dumped over, his mattress had been slit, and everything he owned that would break had been broken.

"Kwok!" I shouted. "Are you okay?"

I went into the front of the store.

Everything my light shone on here was neat as a pin, same as always. Even Paul's shotgun was still in its place beside the sketches.

I found Kwok just in front of his counter. His hand had been broken and a little old Smith & Wesson revolver lay nearby with its barrel smashed off. I wasn't sure what had killed Kwok until I held the lantern to his face and saw his head hanging down like a rag doll's. His neck was broken.

I ran to get Minot.

He wasn't happy about being routed out of bed in the middle of the afternoon, and he made me wait a long time while he put on his uniform and gathered up his notepad and his club.

When he finally came out of his jail looking as if he were ready to go on parade, he started questioning me.

"You are a known associate of this Kwok. You did work for him. What kind of work?" Minot said as we walked to the store.

"Store work," I said. "Whatever he needed."

"And you state that he claimed that the White Wolf owed him money. What proof do you have of that?"

He was jotting down what I told him. The rain was streaking the words on the paper as fast as he took them down.

"Kwok's word," I said. "And the White Wolf is in town, and Kwok's dead. What are you going to do about it?"

"Whatever the law requires," Minot said.

When we got to the store, he opened the shutters and looked all around, more as if he were shopping than gathering evidence. Then he put a handkerchief to his face and stood over Kwok.

"No bullet wounds," he said. "No knife wounds."

"He's had his neck broken, damn you," I said.

Minot lifted Kwok's head with the toe of his boot and let it flop back.

"Ah," he said. "The fatal wound."

Minot put his foot down and started writing again in his little notebook.

"Was he a Christian?" he asked.

"How would I know?" I said. "Anyway, what difference does it make?"

"It makes a difference as to where he is to be buried," Minot said. "We don't want a pagan in the Christian cemeteries."

"What are you going to do about the White Wolf?" I said.

"The evidence against him is purely circumstantial at best," Minot said. "The *Mateata* is in harbor. You say Kwok told you the White Wolf owed him money. Now Kwok is dead. That is all. We do not know if Kwok was already dead before the *Mateata* arrived. Indeed, as the one who claims to have found Kwok here, you are more under suspicion than anyone else. I suppose you will tell me that you took nothing from this store before you came and got me?"

"Search me if you want to," I said, trying hard to keep my temper.

Minot shrugged. "That will not be neccessary. Hold yourself available for further questioning. In the meantime I must take measures for the disposal of the body."

"That's it?" I said. "That's all you're going to do?"

"I shall file the proper reports," he said. "No one attaches much importance to the death of a Chinese merchant."

"I do," I said.

He tilted his chin toward the door. It was my signal to leave.

I went out and stood on the porch while he shut the door and wrote a note that everyone was strongly forbidden to enter. I watched until he was out of sight. Then I entered.

I found some paper and a pen. I wrote a quick note to Jénot:

The men we both know are bad just killed Kwok.
I am going after them now. If you don't hear from me
again, you will know what happened.

Totefa

I slipped the note into the little mailbox by the counter. Then I took down the shotgun, broke it open and slipped in two cartridges from a box nearby. I stuffed another ten or so in my pockets. That should be plenty.

"I'm going to get 'em for you, Kwok; I swear it." I said. "You and Robert."

I went out into the rain-soaked night. What was I going to do next? I decided the best thing would be to hide as close to the *Mateata* as I could, then shoot Gun and the White Wolf as they came back to it. It couldn't be long before they did.

I found some bushes about a hundred yards from the beach close to the path that led to where boats landed. I lay flat, my legs spread out, my shotgun steady. If they just did what I knew they'd do, I couldn't miss.

The rain beat down, and my hat's brim began to uncurl and droop down around my face. I didn't mind. I just wished the White Wolf and Gun would come back so we could get this over with.

At last I heard them coming. Even with the noise of the storm, they were loud. Then I saw why. There were seven of them. And five of them were carrying long, heavy boxes on their backs. The White Wolf was in the lead, and Gun was bringing up the rear.

Seven. I hadn't banked on seven. I didn't want to kill the other five. Push come to shove, I didn't much care about killing the White Wolf. It was Gun I wanted.

Well, I still could. I'd bushwhack him as he passed. I'd aim right at his black-tattooed head. Then whatever happened would happen. I got ready to shoot.

But Smoking Mirror wasn't done with me that day. I had my finger on the triggers, but I was scared and I'd never fired this piece before. I had no way to know that just a little pressure made it go off, and that's what happened. Both barrels exploded, turning the night an ugly yellow-white for just a second and filling the bushes with the sweet stink of gunpowder.

The man just in front of Gun went down screaming. He dropped his heavy crate and it burst open. Old Springfield rifles like Kwok's father's spilled out of it.

Gun turned toward me and charged, whipping out his pistols.

My ears were ringing. I heard the White Wolf shout from far away, but didn't hear the words.

I tried to drag out more cartridges, but the damp cloth of my jeans clutched at them, and before I could reload, Gun was over me.

He stared down at me from above the barrels of his pistols.

"Who the hell you?" he asked in French.

Then the White Wolf shouted something again, and Gun dropped one pistol, held the otehr one on me, and picked up the shotgun. he tossed it away and hauled me to my feet.

"Bring him," the White Wolf said. "Quickly."

Gun dragged me over to where the White Wolf was standing.

"Why did you attack?" he asked, staring into my face. "I don't know you."

"He killed Kwok," I managed to say. "He killed Robert."

"Now I recall you," the White Wolf said. "That day in Papeete. Yes. So Kwok was also a friend of yours? You have a bad habit of choosing friends who cause me trouble. And now you have caused me trouble."

The man I'd wounded was lying on the ground, sobbing and trying to get up. I couldn't believe he was still alive.

"I'm sorry," I blurted out.

He didn't answer, and Gun laughed.

"We must leave these rifles," the White Wolf said. "Even Minot may feel obliged to investigate gunshots. Gun, bring the kanaka."

"You," he said to me. "Take the man's feet."

We hurried down to the boat. I felt lightheaded and excited in a strange way. Maybe it was because of what I'd done. Maybe it was because I knew I was as good as dead.

When we got to the *Mateata,* I was trussed up and thrown into the hold next to the man I'd shot. They laid the rifle cases beside us.

I felt the ship begin to move. Beside me, the man I'd wounded—no, killed. I was sure he was going to die—babbled a few words in Tahitian, fell silent, and babbled again.

I don't know where he thought he was, but he was nowhere near the *Mateata.*

"Philippe, don't take that. It's mine. . . .Oh, there's the other one. . . . What birds? . . . My mother's house . . . My mother's birds . . . water for me . . . water . . ."

I lay there and listened to his voice getting weaker as the *Mateata* wallowed on. Then, after a little while we stopped and I heard the anchors run out. After a time, the hatches opened and more cases of guns were brought down. I smelled land. I reckoned we must be anchored at Moorea.

"This man's dying, he needs help," I said to the other men.

One of them kicked me. That was all the answer I got.

The rain stopped after a while. I guessed it must be about dawn.

The man hadn't spoken in a while. Now he opened his eyes. I wasn't sure he could see me, but he was looking in my direction.

"I'm sorry," I said again, this time in Tahitian.

"Why?" the man asked me.

"It was a mistake. I was aiming for Gun," I said.

"Good," the man said, "You have water?"

His voice was a rough whisper now.

"I'm tied up," I said.

"I'm going now," he said.

And he did.

CHAPTER TWENTY

The *Mateata*

The next day Gun came and got me. He hauled me up on deck and threw me down in front of the White Wolf. Then he yanked me up so I was sitting. My stiffened muscles screamed at me.

"You worked for Kwok," the White Wolf said. "How much do you know about his business?"

"He ran a store in Mataeia. Everybody knows that." I was twisting around, trying to find some position that hurt less.

"That was only part of his business," the White Wolf said. "The rest was illegal. He smuggled guns. I wanted part of that trade, but he refused to deal with me."

"You owed him money," I said.

"Which I would have paid him had he seen fit to use my ship as part of his system of business," the White Wolf went on. "I myself am a merchant in this line when opportunity offers itself. I keep my stock here. But it would be more efficient if one ship handled all the business. I pointed this out to Kwok more than once. When at last I saw there was no way of reasoning with him, I determined to take over the business myself. That involved finding out who was carrying his shipments for him and seeing that they would no longer do so."

Gun, standing behind me, laughed.

I thought of all the times I'd tied red rags to that cocoa palm and knew that had been some kind of signal, and realized now why Kwok had been nervous the last time I'd seen him alive. His contact hadn't come.

"He had another merchant like myself who picked up the rifles and then carried them beyond the twelve-mile limit to rendezvous with clipper ships that took them to China," the White Wolf said. "He had many customers there. Unfortunately, it will not be possible for either of us to profit by his system now. Those rifles we brought aboard in Mataiea will be the last ones. Kwok should have been more reasonable."

He studied me.

"You have cost me a man and a case of rifles," he said. "You owe me a great deal."

"I don't owe you anything," I said.

"You do," the White Wolf said. "And I will have it from you one way or another."

He put his hands together like he was praying.

"Let us see," he said. "I can keep you aboard until you have worked enough to pay me back. Then Gun can kill you. But you seem perhaps a little too dangerous for that."

"Kill him now," Gun said.

The White Wolf shook his head.

"I must have a profit from him," he said. "Wait. I have it. We are already rendezvousing with *The Queen of Kowloon* tomorrow night to resell the rifles. We will include him. The captain will be glad to get an extra hand, and will pay well for him. Then, if Minot or anyone in Papeete should ask, we can say, "Yes, we knew him. He shipped out on *The Queen of Kowloon*. You know the captain of that ship, my friend. Don't you think I've had a good idea?"

"Hell ship," Gun grinned.

"He will die there, sooner or later," the White Wolf said. "If not on this voyage then on another. Take him back down. And bring up that other fellow. It's time we fed the sharks."

They put me back in the hold. Even with the dead man gone, his smell was strong. Like rotting meat, but with something else in it that seemed to dance in my nostrils like a joke. Maybe I was smelling Smoking Mirror.

I lay there that day feeling the bonds on my wrists and ankles tight as fate. The lightheaded feeling I'd had was going away, leaving me alone with my fear and despair. I went down to a lower place than I'd ever guessed existed.

But, after a long time, something began to come into that place and keep me company. It was myself. Myself. Whatever Smoking Mirror had done to me in the past, I'd done this thing on my own. I was down here because of choices I'd made, chances I'd taken. That made me as strong as Smoking Mirror. And if I was as strong as that, I had a chance. Let them stick me aboard their hell ship. Wasn't I in hell right this minute? And there was nothing down here that was bigger than I was.

And if I did live I'd escape when we got to China, and I'd come back to Tahiti. And if Tehane was still here and not married, I'd ask her. Let Paul paint her a hundred times any way he wanted. I still loved her. Do what you want, Smoking Mirror. Totefa's comin' right back at you. That was my thought and my prayer in that dark place.

I think we stayed at Moorea another day, but it's hard to say. I only know when we weighed anchor, it was after sundown. Gun brought me up on deck again and tied me to a stanchion.

"You may as well wait here," The White Wolf said. "It will be easier to exchange you. A beautiful night, is it not?"

The night wind on my skin was like life breathing into me. I lifted my head to the sky.

Overhead it was deep black, filled with stars. The moon was rising out of the sea, and the sky began to glow with its light. I could see Tahiti dark against it, lovely and familiar. We passed her slowly, the sails rustling a deep note that promised something I couldn't understand. I looked at those sails and smiled.

Gun stood over me and grinned. The black tattoo in the middle of his forehead looked bigger tonight.

"Why you smile?" He laughed. "Captain on that ship kill you for us when you get to China."

"Maybe," I said.

Tahiti was growing larger as we changed course for our rendezvous. It looked as if I'd be taken somewhere north of Papeete.

Good-bye, old island, I thought. Don't forget me.

As we made our course change, I heard the sound of a steam engine.

Then, looking behind me, I saw the plume of smoke against the sky.

Was this my ship, I wondered.

Then there was the dull boom of a cannon and the hollow *whoosh* of its shell flying over the *Mateata* and throwing up a plume of white water far ahead of us.

"The *Vire* is after us," I heard someone shout.

I saw Gun jump. I saw the White Wolf run to the stern. He shouted orders, and the *Mateata* turned, trying to make full use of the wind, trying to race the *Vire* for the twelve-mile limit. Beyond that, the White Wolf was safe from any law.

I heard the sound of the *Vire*'s engines working harder, coming closer; and the cannon fired again. This shell passed so close, it sucked air from the sails.

Gun started firing at the *Vire* with a huge, old-fashioned rifle. The White Wolf ordered him to stop; but he went on shooting, just as if he thought he could hurt the gunboat.

I think the White Wolf might have made it if he'd taken better care of his ship. Whatever was making the *Mateata* ride low in the water was slowing her down too much now.

"Throw the cargo overboard," the White Wolf ordered.

But nobody moved.

"The next shot will be aimed at us," one of the crew shouted.

"They won't dare to sink me," the White Wolf said. "Throw the cargo overboard."

But instead the men dropped the sails on the mainmast. Gun dropped his rifle and pulled out his pistols, but the White Wolf put himself in front of their muzzles.

"We are caught now," he told Gun. "Revenge must wait."

A few minutes later the *Vire* was alongside. I raised my head over the rail and saw a big rowboat with a squad of marines heading toward us.

"I order you to permit me to board at once," shouted Lieutenant Jénot.

"Of course, Jénot," the White Wolf answered. "Forgive me for running. I thought you might be pirates."

"If there is a pirate here, it is not I," Jénot said.

The rowboat tied up to us, and Jénot came over the side with his sword drawn.

The first man after him was Paul Gauguin.

He still had on his beret, but he was wearing the striped shirt and wide trousers of a French seaman. He had a cutlass in his hand, a deck under his feet, and blood in his eyes. What a sailor he must have been. What a man he was. What a warrior.

The marines swarmed over the ship, and two of them held the White Wolf under guard while Jénot inspected everything on deck.

But Paul had come on other business. He was here for me.

"Free him at once!" he shouted. "Cut those bonds."

But Gun was reaching for his pistols.

"No," he said. "He dies."

Paul let out a war cry and leaped across the deck in one of the fencing moves I'd seen him do that day in front of our place. One of Gun's pistols went off, and Paul stabbed him at the same moment. For a few seconds more, Gun stood there, looking surprised. Then

Paul gave him a heave and he went over backward into the sea with Paul's cutlass still in him.

Paul found a knife and cut me loose. He helped me to stand.

"How badly hurt are you?" he asked.

"Not too bad," I said. "Only about half dead."

Meanwhile, Jénot was talking to the White Wolf.

"I find some irregularities here," Jénot said. "There are cases of rifles aboard, and a man in bonds but not in the brig. Explain."

"The weapons are legitimate cargo," the White Wolf said. "I am merely transferring them to another ship. As for the man, take him with you if you wish. He killed one of my crew. He is a criminal."

"I will take him," said Jénot. "He is an agent of mine. But to return to the weapons. They are of two kinds. One set of cases may be legitimate, but the others appear to be some that were stolen from the arsenal in Papeete. How did you come by those?"

"I did not come by anything," the White Wolf said. "I was given those cases to transport by the merchant Kwok in Mataeaia. Ask him how he came by them."

"Kwok is dead," Jénot aid. "But I expect you know that."

"I had not heard," the White Wolf said.

"Liar," I hissed.

"I am taking your ship in to Papeete," Jénot aid. "You can make your explanations in court."

"I am eager to explain everything," the White Wolf said. "I am only a legitimate businessman."

"Manacle him," Jénot said, and a corporal came forward with a set of handcuffs.

Paul was standing beside me, holding me up. I hugged him as tightly as I could.

"I hope I have acted as you would have done," he said. "My noble savage."

"I sent Jénot a note," I said. "But what are you doing here?"

"When you disappeared I went to Papeete to look for you," Paul said. "I arrived the same day as your note and went to see Jénot. He didn't want to bring me. But I pointed out that I have never been discharged from the French navy. Then I volunteered."

"I did well to bring you," Jénot said. "You are worth a squad."

Paul grinned. Then his face went pale, and he let go of me. I staggered back as he fell to his knees and vomited blood on the deck.

When he was done at last, he gasped, "It is not so bad, Totefa. I have had it before. It started again on the day you left. Now you are back, perhaps it will stop."

But it didn't.

CHAPTER TWENTY-ONE

Hospital

Jénot left most of the marines aboard the *Mateata* and the *Vire* took her under tow. Then we headed back to Papeete at full speed.

On the way back Paul felt a little better. He sat up, leaning against me while Jénot asked me to tell him what I knew about the White Wolf and Kwok's death.

"Unfortunate in every way," Jénot said when I was done. "Kwok was my chief agent in Mataiea. I had no idea he was also running guns. That will certainly complicate my efforts to bring the White Wolf to trial."

"Who were the guns for?" I asked.

"It does not matter," Jénot said. "There are always those who want guns." He sighed and said, "I had hoped to send the White Wolf to Devil's Island. Now I doubt he will even come to trial. He is well connected in Papeete, and his friends will try to protect him. Ah, well, perhaps being dragged back to town in chains will put some fear in him. He may go back to cheating the natives on the outer islands, which is his natural level of criminality."

I shook my head. Not everyone pays what he owes.

When the launch reached Papeete, it was nearly dawn and the sky was red and gold. The clouds sailing by looked too precious for earth.

Under that beauty the three of us made our way to the hospital. Jénot gave the hospital twenty francs for his first day's stay. Then he took me to breakfast at the Cercle Militaire.

"At twenty francs a day, he will not be able to stay long at the hospital," Jénot said. "I can afford to help him for only a few days."

"I have some money too," I said. "Maybe enough for a week. But what's wrong with him?"

Jénot shook his head.

"I am not a doctor," Jénot said. "But he did the same thing once in Papeete. He told me then that there were several diseases with his symptoms and that none of them were pleasant. He may simply be put on a strengthening treatment and then released. It is probably all that can be done."

I remembered the times he'd staggered or sagged and I'd thought he was just tired or drunk. He'd been fighting this. And it sounded as if a few hundred francs might be all that he'd need to be well again. It might as well have been a million dollars. Poor Paul. Poor brave, tough, sneaky Paul with his paint and his dreams of a savage paradise and his longing for greatness. *Que hombre,* I thought. What a man.

That afternoon I went to see Paul. The hospital was a big, white, airy place, and the hospital was taking good care of Paul.

"Ah, Totefa," he said. "We have had a great adventure, no?"

I just sat down and took his hand.

"Do not worry," Paul said. "I am not going to die of this."

"Listen, Paul," I said. "Jénot's going to cover the first few days. I'm going to go back home and get the rest of my money. You can have all of it."

"Well, I should like to stay here until I am well; but I don't think that will happen," Paul said. "When the money runs out, I will leave here and go back to Mataiea. God will spare me for a time yet. He knows how much work I have to do."

I didn't like to hear Paul taking like this. It wasn't like him to be so philosophical. I wanted to hear him get mad or sarcastic about something. Then I'd know he was getting well.

But he didn't. Instead he started talking about everything under the sun. About art, his family, his plans to go to New Zealand some-day and see their carvings. And I felt myself carried along on his words, as always.

By the end of visiting hours he almost sounded strong again.

A nurse came through and said it was time to go. I stood up.

"When will you leave for Mataiea?" Paul asked.

"I think maybe I'll go tonight," I said. "Walk there in the cool dark, catch some sleep, and start back tomorrow."

"My savage," he said, and smiled as sweetly as a child. "When you come back, please bring my pencils and sketchbook."

The road to Mataiea seemed familiar and new at the same time. Everything I saw I'd seen before, and everything I'd seen before looked as though someone had polished it just for me. After a few miles I'd walked the pain from my ropes out of my legs and arms, and after that I almost felt as if I were floating in the the shining dark.

It was past midnight when I reached Mataiea. Everything was quiet. The *himene* singers were asleep; the parties were over. The little lights were shining in the windows where women slept alone.

I reached the place I shared with Paul and stopped. There was a light burning there too.

I went in and saw Tehane asleep on the floor. She was stretched out on some canvas with her arm over her face, and in the flickering lamp glow she was more beautiful than she'd ever been.

Propped up behind her was the painting Paul had named *Matamoe*. There I was, raising my ax over the silvery wood, chopping away everything dead and useless, making it swirl away in white smoke where the clouds were waiting to take it in and carry it away. That was how he saw me.

I looked at it for a long time, taking it in. I didn't move until Tehane turned over, saw me, and sat up.

"I have been waiting a long time for you to come back," she said.

"A lot has happened," I said. "More than I can tell you right now."

"When you saw me that day and ran away," she said. "I want you to know why I let him paint me like that." Her eyes were on the floor, and she was talking fast. "I only did it because I wanted you to see the painting. I hoped it would make you jealous."

I didn't say anything. I just knelt down and held her.

It was a long while before either of us said anything else.

As the sun was coming up, I told her everything that had happened to me since I'd seen her last.

"He saved you," she said. "He is a good man after all."

"He's just Paul," I said. "Like a lion's just a lion. They do what they do."

"When he comes back, will you go on living with him?"

"No," I said. Then I said, "I love you, Tehane. Will you marry me?"

She held me again, and I looked again at *Matamoe,* and I knew what Paul had painted had become real. I'd cut away my fear of Smoking Mirror and sent it up into the clouds. The next time he came to me, he'd find himself facing a man.

CHAPTER TWENTY-TWO

¡Viva!

I didn't go back to Papeete that day. I sent Paul's money to him on the mail coach instead. There was too much going on in Mataiea for me to do anything else.

It was Minot who changed my plans for me. He came over to my place late that morning and told me there was something Kwok had left me waiting at the police station. When I went to see what it was, I took Tehane along.

"This was found among his papers," Minot said. "I have opened it as you can see. Since it is not evidence in the case, you may have it now."

It was a letter.

> *Dear Joe,*
>
> *I'm writing this just in case things get bad for me in the next few days. I won't bore you with details. You've been a good friend, and you've never asked too many questions. This is good-bye.*
>
> > *So long,*
> > *Ulysses Kwok*

P.S. Since you always wanted a gun, take the old Springfield from the wall above the counter. Be careful when you clean it. Do a good job.

"He gave me his daddy's rifle," I said.

"Then go and take it," Minot said.

I didn't have any use for it now, but I still thought I might keep it since it came from Kwok.

Slowly and sadly I went over to the store and got down the old thing. It weighed about as much as a cannon and wasn't a whole lot smaller, but I took it home to clean it as Kwok had wanted.

When I got it apart, I found a string hanging out of the breech. I thought it must be part of the cleaning gear; but when I pulled on it, a small roll of currency came out. I yanked again, and there was another. I kept on pulling until a string as long as the rifle's barrel was in my hand. I started unwrapping the bills; and by the time I was done, I had five thousand dollars in my hands.

Five thousand dollars? Five thousand dollars! It was blood money, for sure. Kwok had gambled his life for those greenbacks, and he had lost. He'd saved it and hoarded it. He'd hoped to spend it on—what? I'd never know. But he wanted me to have it, and I intended to use it well. There were places in California where I could get a thousand acres of land and have money left over. Tehane and I would have our own place, where we'd raise our kids and be beholden to no one. And I would never be alone again—never alone the way Kwok had been.

I ran to her house with the money stuffed in my pockets.

She was sitting under the trees petting her old dog when I came up to her, gasping.

"Look, Tehane," I said. "We're rich. Near rich, anyhow. I can take you home. We'll get our own land. Be independent."

She studied the bills without touching them.

"This is what you want?" she said. "To leave Tahiti?"

"Not just leave Tahiti," I said. "Go to California. You'll like it there."

"But will it like me?" she said. "Did it like you? We may own land, but will white people respect us and our children?"

"Some will, some won't," I said. "The point is, it won't matter. When you have your own place, you're someone."

"I have a place here," she said. "I am someone now."

"You saying you want to stay?" I said.

"My father always said I should see more of the world than this litle island," she said. "But he meant that I should go to France. I always thought I would, one day."

We stood there under the cocoa palms just looking at each other.

Finally, Tehane said, "Come with me."

We walked up the trail to the *marae* her clan had built long ago, when the Tahitian people had filled their island, and sung to their old gods in their coral temples.

When we got there, she stood a long time looking up at the bare top of the old pyramid. I took her hand and waited.

"They say it is right for me to go," she said at last. "Our blood will not die out in the land. They say it is good to carry our blood to a new country."

"California's just part of my country," I said.

"You are my country now," she said.

After that everything happened pretty fast. Maria made Tehane's wedding dress. I told Anani I was leaving and why, and he bought our steamer tickets as a wedding present. We set a date, and Tehane invited every relative she had from all over the island. I invited Anani, Jénot, and Paul.

Paul was back from the hospital in time, looking pale but seeming to be okay. He came to the wedding wearing the suit he'd kept for going back to France. But he wore his beret with it, with a peacock feather on one side, and he kept it on in church. I was glad to see that. It meant he really was feeling better.

At the party he took off his suit and danced wearing a *pareo* cloth. He sang French songs and Spanish ones, playing his guitar. When the fire had burned down and everyone had eaten and drunk everything there was, he fell asleep under a tree.

Then Tehane and I went into her mother's house as man and wife.

The next day I walked with Paul back to our place one last time.

"The little friends will be lonely for you," he said.

I knew what he meant by that, and it raised a lump in my throat.

"Paul, you've been the best shipmate I ever had," I said. "Even better than Robert."

"You have been more to me than I can say, Totefa," Paul said. "Good-bye."

Suddenly he turned and hugged me there on the road.

"Don't come any farther with me," he said, and I saw there were tears in his eyes. "My best respects to Madame Sloan."

I watched him walk the rest of the way to our house. When he was so far away I didn't know if he could hear me or not, I raised my big brown Stetson from my head and waved it.

"*¡Viva el hombre salvaje!*" I shouted. "*¡Viva el artista grande! ¡Viva Gauguin!*"

Then I turned and walked to where Tehane was waiting.

Paul Gauguin's Life and Art

The great unifying theme of twentieth-century intellectual life was the search for ultimate origins. Physical scientists asked questions about the origins of the universe, of man, and of life itself. Psychiatrists and psychologists looked for the basic elements of human personality. Many writers and artists undertook to express this in their own ways.

Although he barely lived into the twentieth century, Paul Gauguin expressed this search in paint and sculpture. From the time he first visited Tahiti in 1891, his art was filled with work that attempted to answer the question posed in the title of one of his greatest paintings: *What Are We? Where Do We Come From? Where Are We Going?* (Boston Museum of Fine Arts). It is as if he announced the coming of the new century and its mighty quest.

Paul Gauguin was an improbable man for this work. He had been a poor student, excelling only in fencing. He had failed the exams for the French naval academy and joined the merchant marine as a common seaman. He was discharged after France lost the

Franco-Prussian War of 1870-71 and never returned to the sea. He only began to study painting when he was in his twenties, and at first he seemed to be destined to become nothing more than a "Sunday painter." He had a family to support, and he was making a good living working on the Paris stock exchange. It was only after he lost his job in the stock market crash of 1883 that he turned to art as a career. He then determined not only to make a living from his work, but to turn himself into a great artist.

Remarkably, he succeeded. In the 1880s he painted in France, and never went anywhere more exotic than Brittany, where the peasants would put on their traditional costumes and pose for painters who could pay them. But even then, Gauguin was thinking of setting up a studio somewhere overseas in the French empire where there would be warmth, cheap living, and exotic scenes to paint, scenes that would recall the spiritual purity of the uncorrupted civilized world in which he believed. Gauguin placed great importance on his Peruvian ancestry, a connection made through his maternal grandmother. Because of it, he considered himself to be something of a "noble savage."

He tried the Caribbean island of Martinique in the late 1880s. Then he decided on Tahiti, a place he knew only through a popular novel called *The Marriage of Loti*. He went there in 1891 for about six months, the period in which *Smoking Mirror* is set.

Instead of the primitive idyll he had imagined, he found that French colonialism had already spread its mark there. Nevertheless he still found in it the inspiration he sought. Within a few months he was creating works that were a synthesis of what he was seeing, what he had already learned about different styles of art, and what he imagined. His paintings from the South Pacific are what he saw when he did.

During that first visit, he met many of the people mentioned in this story. Lieutenant Jénot, Titi, Anani, Tehura, and the White Wolf were all real. There were also a Chinese merchant with whom Gauguin traded and a police officer with whom he got in trouble for bathing nude, but their names are made up. Tehane, Anapa, and Gun are completely fictional.

Whether Totefa existed or not is a mystery. After Gauguin's death, many people went out to Tahiti and the Marquesas to speak to those who had known him. None of them seem to have met Totefa, or to have talked to anyone who knew him. The only source for his existence is Gauguin's personal journal *Noa Noa,* and the five or six paintings from this period in which he appears. Art historians have said that each appearance marks an important shift in Gauguin's work, marking a new depth. He never appears in anything Gauguin painted after he returned to Tahiti from France in 1892.

Matamoe is generally considered the last of the Totefa paintings. But there is one more picture, which was apparently painted just a little later, in which a young man on horseback and wearing a broad-brimmed hat, is seen riding away from Gauguin, who is walking away in the opposite direction. The young man seems to be the same man who was in the portrait of Tehura, the first one in which Totefa appears. This painting has the feeling of good-bye about it.

Possibly Gauguin made him up. But it is also possible that Totefa was someone real, who was just passing through Mataiea and wasn't there when Gauguin came back. It is unlikely that we will ever know.

Gauguin's return to France was brief and bitter. He had a reputation, but it earned him no sales. He was not able to reunite his
family and support them. He returned to the islands of the French
empire and never saw his wife or any of his children again. For the
rest of his life, until he died at the age of fifty-five in 1903, he lived
hand-to-mouth, desperate for cash much of the time, but able somehow to find the money for paint and canvas.

When he died in the Marquesas Islands in 1903, a native friend
found him lying half out of bed. The visitor bent over, and, following
the traditon of his people, bit Gauguin on the forehead to make sure
he was dead.

As soon as he was dead, Gauguin's reputation in the art world
bloomed like a Tahitian tiare. His work began to command the kind
of prices of which he had always dreamed, and today his paintings
hang in museums all over the United States and Europe.

The tough sailor, the ambitious businessman, became the first
great artist of the twentieth century.

A Timeline of Gauguin's Life

1848   Born in France. His father is a liberal journalist. His mother is half-Peruvian.

1850   Gauguin's family moves to Peru. Paul's father dies on the trip.

1854   Paul and his mother return to France.

1865   Paul leaves school and joins the French merchant marine.

1870–1871   Paul is drafted into the French navy. Serves aboard the *Jérome Napoleon*, the personal yacht of Emperor Napoleon III. The yacht is armed for combat and serves in the Franco-Prussian War, which France loses.

1872   Paul begins working at the French stock exchange.

1873   He meets and marries Mette Gad, from Denmark.

1875   The Paris stock exchange, where Paul works, is in the same neighborhood as the best art galleries. He begins to buy paintings, and to study painting under Camille Pissaro.

1876   Paul has a painting included in an important exhibition.

1883   Following a stock market crash, Paul loses his lucrative job. He decides to devote himself to art.

1884   Paul is not able to support his family. Mette takes the children and returns to her family in Denmark.

1885   Paul follows them, but is unable to earn enough to support them there, either.

1885-1888   Paul develops rapidly as an artist, learning to sculpt in clay and to carve as well as to work in the process called zincography. He lives in different parts of France trying to save money. At one point, he works putting up posters for five francs a day.

1888   Paul visits Panama. Tries to work on building the Panama Canal for two weeks, becomes ill, and goes to Martinique. He fantasizes about living cheaply here, as part of a gang of artists.

1890   Moves to Arles in southern France and lives with Vincent van Gogh for three months. They quarrel and Gauguin leaves.

1891   Gauguin goes to Tahiti. Encounters Totefa, whatever that encounter may have been.

1892   Returns to France, but cannot sell his paintings. He returns to the Pacific and never leaves it again.

1892   On the way back to Tahiti he visits New Zealand to study the elaborate art of the Maori people.

1901   Leaves Tahiti for the Marquesas Islands. He is interested in the elaborate stone sculptures he has heard about there.

1903   Dies of syphilis, which he probably contracted while serving in the French merchant marine.

FOR MORE INFORMATION

Readers can learn more about Gauguin's life from:

There are many books about Paul Gauguin, but most of them read like repeats of one another. The errors and opinions of one author tend to get repeated. The two biographies I've listed below had the best detail of any I looked at, and do not agree with each other about the kind of man Gauguin was. I found them both very helpful in writing my own version of the man, who is diffrent from either.

Paul Gauguin; an Erotic Life by Nancy Mowll Matthews (Yale University Press: New Haven, 2001)

Paul Gauguin; a Life by David Sweetman (Simon & Schuster, New York: 1995)

A collection of his works with good commentaries is,

Gauguin; a Retrospective by Marla Prather and Charles F. Stuckey, editors (High Lauter and Associates: New York, 1987)

There are numerous websites devoted to Gauguin, but as always with the Internet, the infomation contained in them tends to be less accurate than the information in books. It is, however, an easy way to look at the paintings.

A teacher's guide to *Smoking Mirror* is available at www.wgpub.com.

TO VIEW THE WORK OF PAUL GAUGUIN VISIT:

The Art Institute of Chicago
Chicago, IL
312-443-3600
www.artic.com

Guggenheim Museum
New York, NY
212-4223-3500
www.guggenheim.org

Hermitage Museum
Saint Petersburg Russia
812-110-96-26
www.hermitagemuseum.org

J. Paul Getty Museum
Los Angeles, CA
310-440-7300
www.getty.edu

Metropolitan Museum of Art
New York, NY
212-535-7780
www.metmuseum.org

Minneapolis Institute of Arts
Minneapolis, MN
612-870-3131
www.artsmia.org

Museum of fine arts
Houston, TX
713-639-7300
www.mfah.org

Museum of Modern Art
New York, NY
212-708-9400
www.moma.org

National Gallery of art
Washington, DC
202-842-6176
www.nga.gov

National Gallery of Canada
Ottawa, Canada
613-990-1985
www.national.gallery.ca

National Gallery of London
London, UK
020-7747-2885
www.nationalgallery.org.uk

Arthur Ross Gallery at the University
of Pennsylvania
Philadelphia, pa
215-898-2083
www.upenn.edu/arg

Cleveland museum of Art
Cleveland, OH
1-888-CMA-0033
www.clevelandart.org

Legion of Honor
San Francisco, CA
415-863-3330
www.thinker.org

Harvard University Art museum
Cambridge, ma
617-495-9400
www.artmuseums.harvard.edu

Indianapolis Museum of art
Indianapolis, IN
317-920-2660
www.ima-art.org

Los Angeles county art museum
Los Angeles, CA
323-857-6000
www.lacma.org

Musee d'Orsay
Paris, France
33-0140-494-814
www.musee-orsay.fr

Museum of Fine arts
Boston, MA
617-267-9300
www.mfa.org

Polish national museum
Warsaw, Poland
48-22-621-10-31
www.mnw.art.pl

Van Gogh Museum
Amsterdam, Netherlands
020-570-5200
www.vangoghmuseum.nl

The Spirit Catchers:
An Encounter with Georgia O'Keeffe
by Kathleen Kudlinski

Like thousands of other Americans during the Great Depression, Parker Ray finds himself homeless and desperate. Now all signs—from his thirst-induced hallucinations to the inhospitable force of nature, Georgia O'Keeffe—tell him that something in the desert is out to get him.

"Kudlinski evokes the extremes of desert life, from desolation to sun-baked beauty, and then depicts the environment's mesmerizing effect on her characters . . . There are enough surprises to keep the pages turning . . . The notion of 'spirit' is woven effectively into a variety of contexts . . ." —*School Library Journal*

"Kudlinski succeeds amazingly at helping her readers look, really look, at the art of Georgia O'Keeffe."—Sam Sebasta, Ph.D., College of Education, University of Washington

". . . the plot takes off partly on the strength of Kudlinski's . . . portrait of O'Keeffe."—*Kirkus Reviews*

". . . the overwhelming feeling at the end is that the reader is 'inside the art, free to comment, and encouraged to experiment.' "—The Historical Novel Society

Hardcover ISBN: 0-8230-0408-2

Price: $15.95

Casa Azul:
An Encounter with Frida Kahlo
by Laban Carrick Hill

When does reality end and fantasy begin? Maria and Victor don't know it yet, but she and her brother may be the key to ending the pain and suffering that ferments inside a magical place, Casa Azul, the home of the painter Frida Kahlo.

Hardcover ISBN: 0-8230-1411-2 price: $15.95

The Wedding:
An Encounter with Jan van Eyck
by E. M. Rees

In fifteenth-century Belgium, young Giovanna Cenami resists an arranged marriage in favor of true love. Who wouldn't choose a handsome and valiant youth over a seemingly dull merchant ten years her senior? Or is there more than meets the eye?

Hardcover ISBN: 0-8230-0407-4 Price: $15.95